INVESTIGATION WRATH

MEL TAYLOR

SEVERN RIVER
PUBLISHING

INVESTIGATION WRATH

Severn River Publishing
www.SevernRiverBooks.com

ISBN: 978-1-64875-558-3 (Paperback)

ALSO BY MEL TAYLOR

The Frank Tower Mystery Series

Investigation Con

Investigation Wrath

Investigation Greed

Investigation Envy

To find out more about Mel Taylor and his books, visit

severnriverbooks.com/authors/mel-taylor

This book is dedicated to all readers. Those who love books.

1

Kinnie Mason dangled one foot over the edge and smiled. She looked out at the water before her, raised her arms and showed her palms to the moon. A whisper of a breeze moved over the ocean, toward Mason, building in intensity, until the zephyr became a gust. She smiled and swiped at her hair, pushing the strands away from a sweaty brow. The quick movement almost sent her over. Mason was standing on the penthouse balcony ledge on the twenty-fifth floor of the Stilton Bay Hotel.

"I can fly," she shouted. "I can fly and watch over my dominion. I am the powerful Kinnie Mason!" She never looked down at the moving dots of people and cars twenty-five floors below her. To her, the park across the street and the office buildings below, all looked like a vast new world, made up of glass, trees, and lights. Her world. She was pleased and held out her arms over the valley as if to grant welcome to everyone below.

Kinnie Mason was naked.

The ledge was one foot wide, made of cement, and firm enough to stand on. Her legs were spread apart, arms wide, allowing the wind to caress her every curve and exposed nipples. "I can fly and breathe fire stronger than a dragon." Her nostrils flared, the pupils of her eyes were tiny. Kinnie's arms waved in the breeze, head lifted slightly upward. To Mason, the streets were her kingdom, ripe with gifts of fruit-bearing trees and gold bricked pathways, all leading to the cobalt ripples of the Atlantic Ocean.

Mason looked down and again slowly dangled one foot over the edge. She was now standing on just her left foot, figuring out how to master this task of flying. She yelled, "All who have business before me, kneel and beg for my attention."

A dark feathered buzzard gave her a passive glance and glided past her. She stared at the bird and paused, as if the flying creature was attempting to speak. The bird disappeared on the night sky, yet she could still hear a command being directed at her. Someone was trying to curry the favor of Queen Mason, trying to divert her energy away from the goal of becoming airborne.

Who would dare approach me unannounced?

Mason tried to ignore the sound. Her full attention was on the kingdom below and soaring above the hovels beneath her.

There, she heard it again. "Go away," she screamed. "Or you will face my wrath."

"Kinnie, please come down." Then, "you'll hurt your voice."

There was too much to be accomplished and the words went by her without an acknowledgment. She reasoned the future of the kingdom was at stake. Mason took a step to her right and felt the wind on her bare breasts. The time to fly was now. Don't wait.

"Kinnie, don't move. Please come down." The voice was much louder now and seemed closer.

"Who approaches me?" Mason spoke over her shoulder, her eyes fixed on the horizon of the charcoal sky and the flat surface of the water. "Who has the nerve to go near the queen."

"Kinnie, er, your majesty, please let me approach. I have important news from the other side of the valley."

She thought about the words and turned to meet the speaker. The voice sounded familiar. He was wearing a blue business suit, white shirt, opened, with striped tie, now pulled out of its knot. He used his hand to swipe a bald head. His hand shook and he looked panicked.

"Kinnie, please come down," he said again.

"Just as soon as I return from my flight."

His jaw twisted into a look of frustration and worry. She was standing there on one foot, poised as if to jump at any second. He tried to make his voice sound confident. "You can't fly just yet. There are thousands of your citizens waiting for you. Please, let me escort you. Your presence is required, your majesty." He stepped forward and extended a hand up to her.

She thought about the request. "Thousands?"

"Thousands."

"Waiting for me?"

"Thousands. They are all waiting for you right now. Please, let me help you into the royal robes." Just a few more inches and he would be touching her fingertips. He inched forward, his fingers out. He held his breath. She now had both feet down on the ledge, reached down and made contact.

In one quick motion, Barry Ruddup managed to pull Kinnie Mason down from the ledge. She collapsed on him and immediately fell into a deep sleep. Ruddup slid his arms under her and picked her up, carrying her back inside the hotel room. He held her for a moment, cradled against him like a bird with a broken wing.

Once she was secure on the couch, he went to the bedroom, snatched up a robe and placed the garment on her. For the first time since he entered the room, he took in a deep breath.

He went back and closed the balcony door. Ruddup looked around for what he should do next. He leaned in close, and made sure she was still breathing.

There was a knock at the door. Ruddup went to answer, never taking his eyes off Kinnie. He opened the door to Jackie Tower.

"C'mon in. She's really bad."

Jackie's eyes were tiny beads under heavy rows of bent brow lines. "Where'd you find her?"

"On the balcony, trying to fly." There was a flatness to his voice, as though he had tried and failed on many other occasions to help her. Ruddup had a habit of making sure to memorize all faces coming into his life. He studied Jackie, recording in his memory the cut above her left eye, the slight puffiness under both eyes that Ruddup assumed would never ever go away. There was a don't-mess-with-me determination in her gait, as though the world stopped being kind to her years ago and she was forcing herself to show a modicum of kindness.

Jackie took her thumbs and gently exposed the brown eyes of Kinnie Mason. "I'm not the doctor…"

"You're the drug rehab expert-" He cut her off.

"Yeah but, I need a doctor to confirm but it sounds like she's on PCP. And from the looks of it, a whole bunch of other stuff. Opioids."

"Well, do what you can. She's supposed to be on a stage performing in twenty minutes."

She looked up at him. "Cancel it."

"I can't."

"Cancel it."

"Do you know what the promoters will do to us?"

"Mister, the only performance she's going to be doing is in the bed, shaking this off. Look at her!"

Ruddup stood there, his eyes scanning the room, checking the time, jaw twitching, as if he was figuring out the next move. "What's the name of your place again?"

"The Never Too Late," Jackie sighed. "You're not thinking about taking her there?"

"I can't and won't check her into a hospital. Too many freakin' photographers. She's supposed to be clean. Just got out of rehab."

"Not my rehab."

"No, out west." He had the look of a man with a plan. "I'll tell the reporters she's gone out of town. I'll call for two cabs. I have a woman on staff who looks like Mason, have her wear her clothes and get into a cab. Once they're gone, we'll take her to your place."

"I don't like this idea. My clients are skittish already. If someone finds out, I'll be mobbed."

Ruddup reached back, like he was going for his wallet. "They won't find out. I really need your help. Money is not an option. We'll pay triple the normal."

The wrinkles in Jackie's brow smashed into one solid worry line.

Jackie said, "Under one condition."

"Name it."

"She goes the second, and I mean the second anyone finds out and shows up with a camera."

"Deal. I'll get everything started. And thanks."

He looked down at Kinnie Mason and pride filled his chest. "Five gold albums," he started. "Three platinum, seventeen weeks with one hit at the top of the charts, and five years of sold out concerts. But she hasn't performed in more than a year. This was going to be her return concert. The only thing stopping her, is herself.

Kinnie opened her eyes for just a moment and reached out her right hand, directing it by memory toward the drawer in the night stand. Her fingers pulled open the drawer and pulled out a bottle of top class Vodka. Before she could work on opening the top, Jackie pulled the bottle out of her hands.

The bottle was eased down on the soft carpet. Jackie looked at Ruddup. "We've got a lot of work to do."

2

Kinnie Mason was awake and running her fingers over the rough surface of the sheets. The bed was pushed into the corner of the room. The place reminded Mason of a dorm room, only less. The floor was tiled and recently polished. The small closet was empty, ready for a new stash of clothes. In the rush, Ruddup forgot to bring anything. Kinnie was wearing stretch jeans and the pink bikini top that she insisted on, and she was instructed to stay in her room.

Words were spoken to her, yet she didn't hear them, still caught in the down-slide of the high. For Mason, she didn't want to hear from anyone. Don't mess with the high and hold on to it as long as possible, she reasoned. Her name was directed her way five times before Kinnie recognized she was being addressed.

Jackie stepped around until she was directly in Mason's face. "Entry here is a two-step process. Your manager is doing step one. He is filling out the paperwork for you to be here." Jackie produced a legal-sized pad and sat down. She used her hand to direct Mason to the other chair in the room.

Jackie took out a pen. "Part two is not so easy. Kinnie, we have to talk. And you have to be honest with me. What I'm going to ask you is what drugs you take, how often, what alcohol you consume, and how much. Do you understand?"

"You're messn' with my buzz," Mason stammered.

"If you don't want to be here, you're free to go. Your manager called me. He said you were ready for this. Are you ready to cut all ties to your drug past and move forward?"

The silence between them was as thick as a concrete wall. "I guess I do."

"You guess?" Jackie swiped her hand over the pad. "How about your drug use?"

"My pills? Yes. All kinds. I need them."

"How often?"

Mason bunched up her face. "At least twice a day. Maybe more, depending on how I'm feeling."

Jackie was writing. "How many pills a day?"

"I don't know."

"Ten pills? Fifteen?" Jackie tried to keep the calm in her voice.

"Yes, that sounds about right. Closer to fifteen."

"And alcohol?"

"I drink vodka."

"Any other pills?"

"Yeah."

"Yeah?"

Kinnie Mason rolled her tongue over a dry cracked lower lip. "I took something, I don't even know what it was, but I won't take it again. Had me thinking..."

"You could fly?"

"Yeah, something like that." Kinnie Mason got up from her chair and started pacing around the room.

Jackie sensed what was wrong. "There are no drugs here for me to give you."

"I can't let this happen."

"Let what happen, Kinnie? You mean an end to using drugs?"

"I can't let that happen."

Jackie got up and stood in her path, blocking any forward movement.

"The first thing you have to do is realize this world you built up has a foundation made of drugs. That's very unstable. You need a solid footing. A place to establish what you think about yourself and I can help you with that."

Mason grabbed Jackie's arms. "I don't think I can do this. I didn't ask to come here."

"That's right, your manager asked a favor. To let you in. Normally, you'd have to come in voluntarily and clean at least one day. Since you were on a balcony ledge, if the police came, he felt it would be a national story. He's trying to be discrete about this. You need to help him and yourself by taking treatment seriously."

Mason sat back down in the chair. "I tried rehab once before. Stayed like two hours. Did not work. My body needs the pills."

"Who is directing your life? The pills, or you?"

Mason sat down and listened to the sounds of the rehab center. She heard the scuffs of feet moving outside in the hallway. A few times Mason heard the raised voices of scattered conversations somewhere in the building, yet she could not make out what was being said. In a regular setting, she would turn it all into words and music. Mason had that ability. She could pick up on the vibe, turn it over in her head and direct her feelings into fingertips and tap out a song.

Right now, her feelings were jammed into a mash-up of fried thoughts and a hunger that drove her to any lengths to find more pills. Nothing else mattered. Just find the damn pills.

"Kinnie?" Jackie whispered. "Are you listening to me?"

"I just need some time."

Jackie got up and walked to the door. "That's what we can give you here. Time. This is a good place. Let us help you." Jackie reached the door and stopped. "My office is just down the hallway. If you need the detox room, we'll get you in there. For now, just rest."

Jackie left the room, but did not close the door all the way. Kinnie Mason stepped to the window and stared at the tree just outside. A bird flittered from one branch to the next, and finally flew off toward a bank of clouds. Freedom, she thought, was just outside, away from the prying questions and the demands to take away her pills. Questions moved through her on what she should do. I can do just what that bird is doing, reasoned Kinnie. *I want to fly, just like that bird.*

3

Franklin Jim-Jim Camen waited for the sixteen-feet-tall wrought-iron gate to swing open before driving the Mercedes onto the roadway, made up of tiny paving stones. He got out of the car, admiring the only home in Stilton Bay with such a driveway. His shoes crunched with each step he made toward the seven-room house. Before reaching the porch, Camen paused for a moment to look over his shoulder.

He had a notion.

The same notion that kept him from trusting anyone in his life. No girl-friends. A few jobs, yet he never invited any co-workers home. Camen made a practice of looking over his shoulder, always ready for an encounter that never happened. He made a habit of going into a place and out the back door, only to re-enter again, just as a precaution. The art of staying in the shadows became his passion. He could do this all by himself. No need for anyone else. Not now. Not ever.

The house had everything he imagined. The front door was gray in color, steps made of granite. Three locks on the door and a security system with all the upgrades gave him that extra ounce of confidence. A feeling of safety. Today, as any other day, Camen went from room to room, listening for any movement. The same routine he maintained for the past seven years. Ever since he made the break.

Protected by stormproof glass and seven outside cameras, Camen could not shake the strong feeling enveloping his mind and body. He looked out through the ceiling to floor windows, watching for any sign of movement. The notion.

Nothing.

The AC had stopped. Camen paid no attention. Eventually, the air-conditioning unit would shut off once the desired temp was reached. He tried a light switch. No lights. Camen checked the television. The twenty-foot screen, covering one wall, did not come on. He went from appliance to appliance and found nothing worked. The cell phone was on the table some thirty feet away. He flipped the light switch on and off several times, as if that would make the power magically come back.

Camen took three steps toward the phone and stopped. He heard a noise. His mind focused on where the sound came from inside the massive house. He stood there, frozen, making as little sound as possible and removed his right shoe. He carefully placed the one-thousand dollar imported loafer on the floor, quietly. Then the left. Just as he was about to make another step toward the phone, he heard the noise again. Was it in back of him? To the side? Camen could not tell.

Instead of the cell phone, he turned to the front door. Just get to the outside. Run!

Camen took three quick steps toward the heavy wooden door, and reached for the first of three locks. A hand grabbed him by the neck and threw him across the floor. "Going somewhere?"

It took two shakes of the head before Camen's vision came into clarity. The figure was large, perhaps six-feet-five, with a left shoulder that dipped lower than the right. The gun in his hand, looked long.

"I can get you money," Camen pleaded. "I have a floor safe. You can have it all."

"I'm not here for the money." The figure moved closer. Camen could now see the weapon had a silencer.

"If you're not here for the money..." Camen thought about getting to his feet. "Why?"

"Why?" There was a rasp to his voice, like someone who once went through packs a day, then gave up smoking. Camen noticed something.

Two details, that sent raw chills through him. The large man was wearing gloves and surgeon-like booties covering his shoes.

"Anything you want, I'll pay it, do it." Camen got to his knees, then stood up.

"Think back. You know why I'm here." The crystal, razor eyes of the figure stayed honed-in on Camen.

Gut-punch fear swept through Camen. "But that was, what, seven years ago. I thought they forgot about me."

The figure said, "They don't forget. You know that. Not after what you did."

"Please, let me disappear. I can triple anything they gave you."

The figure did not budge.

Camen searched his eyes, looking for a common bond, a way to slow him down and process an alternative. All Camen saw were blank, dead eyes as though compromise was never going to be an option.

The gunman moved into position in a way to cut off any escape routes.

Camen jumped over a couch, seeking cover, and made a move to run to the back door, hoping the

figure would miss. When he stood up to run, a big hand grabbed him a second time. Camen was face down, staring at the rug.

"Think about what you did." The figure eased the barrel to the neck of Camen.

"Just let me go. I'll do whatever-"

Camen ripped through his thoughts, trying to come up with the right words to stay alive. There was so much he still wanted to do. There was the planned trip to Alaska and the fishing venture to South America. Camen even thought, now was the time to go out on a date, pull someone into his isolated world. He felt the barrel pull away from the back of his head. Camen braced himself.

Two soft bursts and Camen was silent. The figure stood up to admire the kill. Taking his time, he rolled Camen over on his back. Without any hesitation, he reached down and patted the soft tissue just under Camen's chin, the area just above the Adam's apple. The figure reached into his pocket and pulled out an ice pick and bent down close to the prone body of Franklin Camen.

4

"Jackie! What's wrong?" Jackie ran past the front desk clerk, moving from room to room.

"Dammit," she whispered to herself. Jackie checked the meeting room, the doctor's office, and now the long row of doors leading to sleep quarters. She went to the unoccupied rooms first, hoping to maintain a calm level and not upset the clients. Finally, Jackie returned to the front desk. The clerk looked into Jackie's eyes.

"Have you seen anyone leave since you got here?" Jackie's gaze was directed toward the front door.

"No." The clerk's eyes moved to the same direction as Jackie. "Who are you looking for? What's wrong?"

"We had a Jane Doe check in last night." Jackie's voice trailed off, as she moved to the door as she spoke.

"Jane Doe?" The clerk looked confused.

"Jane Doe. We had to use an assumed name. I can't explain why yet. But, I lost her."

The clerk said, "If she used a back door, the alarm would have gone off."

"I know," Jackie looked frustrated. "It had to be the front door, or..." Jackie disappeared down the hall, to the room being used by Kinnie Mason. A few minutes later, Jackie returned.

"She used the window. It's closed now, but I can tell, it was opened." Jackie pounded the counter. Through the glass of the front door, they saw a car drive up.

"Shit," Jackie hissed.

"Who is that?"

"Trouble."

Barry Ruddup got out of his Mercedes, looking like a man concerned about leaving his car parked in the shadow of the I-95 Expressway. Just as he was about to enter the building, a man stepped in front of him, and blocked his path.

Jackie could not hear the words spoken between them. She stayed positioned near the counter. The man opened the door for Ruddup.

"This man here to see-ya," the man said. "Tole him he's in in the wrong neighborhood."

"It's okay," Jackie said. "I know him."

"Okay." The man walked away.

Ruddup looked cautiously before entering the lobby. "C'mon in," Jackie said, "We don't bite."

He turned and watched the man pick something up off the ground and stuff it into his pocket.

Jackie said, "That's T-Shake."

"T-Shake?" Ruddup looked over the counter at the clerk.

"T-Shake was once one of the best linebackers to come out of high school. Had more scholarships than anyone in the state of Florida."

"Or the country," the clerk corrected.

Jackie looked at the clerk and smiled. "Like I said, a lot of scholarships." She stared out the door. "T-Shake got injured, got hooked on pain pills, then her-in..."

"Heroin," said the clerk.

"Yeah, her-ro-in," Jackie said slowly. "Lost his scholarship, got kicked out of school, family turned their back on him. I found him sleeping out there one morning."

"And today?" Ruddup asked.

"Today he is clean. He was in my program for almost two years." Jackie pointed to him. "If you're asking why he's still here, it's because he won't leave and I'm not about to push him away. He has a job at night, spends his mornings kicking out the transients, and getting rid of garbage. Says he is trying to pay me back for helping him. I give him a few bucks."

"I'm here to check on..." he paused.

"Jane Doe?"

"Yes."

Jackie paused for almost fifteen seconds. "I don't know where she is right now. She got out overnight."

"Got out!" Ruddup's words echoed down the long hallway.

"I would ask you to be quiet. My people are trying to cope. Yelling makes for a bad day."

Ruddup lowered his voice. "I trusted you. She is worth thirty million dollars. And you don't know where she is?"

The eyes of the clerk were as big as saucers. Jackie pulled him aside. "Do you know where she usually goes? Friends?"

Ruddup put his hands on his sides. "You're not the first one."

"First one?"

"First one to lose her." Ruddup rolled his eyes at the ceiling. "Lost her one night, minutes before a television interview. When she arrived, I wish she had stayed away. Could smell her breath a mile away."

They both heard a car pull up outside. T-Shake greeted the car. Kinnie Mason stepped out of a cab. She wore the same pink bikini top and the pasted-on jeans. Mason stepped past a gawking T-Shake, shading her eyes from the blast of the sunrise. She stopped at the door, took in a chest full of roasted air and walked directly up to Jackie.

"I messed up, I know it." She stood there, as if waiting for an inspection.

"Where have you been?" Ruddup leaned in.

"No, I haven't been drinking." She turned back to the cab driver. "Can you pay him? I don't have any cash." Ruddup shrugged and went out the door, reaching for his wallet as he walked toward the cab. She turned to Jackie.

"Yes, I got out through the window." Mason adjusted the bikini top.

"You been using?" Jackie's eyes bored into Mason's pinhole-sized pupils.

"I plead the fifth."

"This isn't a court of law; this is my center. If you break the rules and leave without permission, you are out."

Ruddup came back into the lobby just as Jackie was finishing her tirade. "Please, don't give up on her after just one night."

"To be honest, it was just a few hours." Jackie's voice mellowed just a bit. "Listen, we're here to help you. This is a two-way thing. You, us, working to heal and hear you, get you into single and group counseling, shut down the urges, get you to see a different way of operating so that you don't re-abuse. I've been there, I know. My thing was crack."

"I'm supposed to wilt and fall down at your feet?" Mason pulled out a small mirror from her purse.

"I look like shi-"

Jackie bellowed, "You look like someone who needs help."

"Can you give her one more chance?" Ruddup ran his fingers over his bald head.

Jackie let her hands rest on her hip. "We have a strict rule. One day sober to get in here. I broke that rule when I took you in yesterday, and you went out a window. If my clients heard about that, they would know I'm now easy. I don't care how much money you're worth, you've got to come back tomorrow, clean. What are you on now? Opiates?"

Mason smiled. "I love my pills. I was invited to a party in Stilton Bay. I went."

"She won't do it again." Ruddup was reaching into his wallet again. "She has a recording session next week."

"Don't bother with the money. Clean up, Kinnie. See me tomorrow and we'll talk."

A resigned Ruddup opened the door, directing her to the parking lot. "Where are we going?" Mason asked.

"My house."

Jackie searched the eyes of Kinnie Mason. "What are you afraid of? Withdrawal? I can help you through that. You'll feel muscle ache, maybe cramping, like the flu ten times over, just a general sickness. But I can get you through it. And then recovery."

Kinnie Mason took a look at the clerk, then back at Jackie. "I'm not ready for this."

She walked out the door, followed closely by Ruddup. He kept looking back, still shrugging his shoulders like a man sinking in quicksand.

Jackie watched them get into Ruddup's car and drive off. Outside, T-Shake waited until they left, then entered the lobby.

"I saw her," he said.

"Saw who?" Jackie reached into her pocket for something to write on.

"Down the street. The woman who just left. She looks familiar. Anyway, she had a long talk with him down the block. Long talk."

"Him?"

"Yeah, Jackie. Him. And you're not gonna like it."

5

As the drops turned into a half-glass of poured wine, Sekane Walker smiled. He checked his watch. The two dinner guests would be here in an hour. Plenty of time to prepare the steaks for the grill. He rubbed down the rib-eyes with salt and garlic powder and brushed on some marinade before placing them under a plastic wrap in the fridge.

He walked past a bay window, and the view of the three-acre estate, with a curved driveway leading to the road. When he reached the bathroom, he turned the water on full blast to wash his hands. The dress would be casual; jeans, a black safari shirt, a decade-old pair of loafers and no sox.

He opened his laptop and checked on his stocks. A smile almost wrapped around his head. His portfolio had grown faster than expected and he fought off the urge to revel in his riches. Rather, he thought it best to take a portion and make a few donations to causes, take the humble road. Sekane knew he made the right decision nine years earlier when he broke away. Going it alone was best for him. He just had to keep his guard up.

The clothes were on the bed, ready for a change after a long shower. He stepped through the house looking for any changes that needed his attention before they all arrived.

A black shadow moved past the bay window, unnoticed.

After the shower, Sekane got into the jeans and splashed on a nice smell before donning the shirt.

Outside, the figure moved to the back of the house and stood for a moment near the rear door. Rather than attempt a door breach, he pulled out a rope ladder from a duffle and tossed the soft ladder up and against the patio screen covering the pool. A gas grill was all set up with cooking utensils and a towel. The figure pulled on the ropes, letting two hooks cut through the screen mesh. He now had a way to the roof. The climb up took just seconds. Wearing slipper-like booties and gloves, he walked in quick easy steps to the two large sky lights just over the kitchen. He pulled the duffle from around his shoulder and pulled out a cutting tool. The cuts severed the bond between the sky light and its grip on the roof. He pulled the covering off and placed it on the roof. More seconds were needed to make sure he was not detected.

Quiet.

The figure lowered his body through the opening and he dropped to the kitchen floor soft as a giant cat, catching the duffle before the bag hit the counter.

Sekane finished dressing. He walked into the family room next to the kitchen and felt a draft. The short walk between the room has been one he'd made a few thousand times since he bought the house eleven years ago, yet he didn't remember a draft hitting him when he approached the kitchen. He stopped. Beside the wind draft, he could hear the language of crickets with more clarity than ever. Sekane back-stepped into the bedroom, reaching the nightstand within seconds, pulling out the drawer and reaching for the Glock. Now armed, he again made his way into the open part of the house.

The barrel of the gun went first. Sekane stayed behind his aim, moving his sight from left to right, scanning the room for any intruder.

"Come out now and you won't be hurt." Sekane yelled into the cavity of the house. He took another step. Before his right foot touched the floor, the kick landed against the back of his neck, sending him sprawling downward and the gun sliding across the sheen of the wooden planks. Sekane never got the chance to turn. Another kick to the jaw shut down his will to get up. He just rested there, face up and now he could see the missing sky light.

He heard the voice before he saw the large figure.

"You know why I'm here, don't you?"

Thoughts cascaded through his head. "But that was a long time ago," Sekane said. He started to reach back and check the wounds to his face.

"Don't move!"

He obeyed. "Look," he started. "I moved on. It's time we all forgot about the past."

"They don't forget. Ever. You, of all people should know that."

Options. Sekane's brain rambled through a plan of escape. How to get away.

"Is there anything we can do to stop this?" Sekane put his hands up, then dropped them. There was probably time for one last plea. But what would he say?

The big man sighed. "I have one more stop before I rest. You're just one thing I have to do."

"No! You don't have to do anything." More than anything, Sekane wanted to move his head. The figure's voice was coming from a different part of the house. He was moving around, getting into position. Time was running out.

"They wanted you to think about this for a moment before it happens."

"Please, stop this."

"You want it to stop? I need something. Information."

"Anything. Just tell me. What is it?"

The figure lowered the gun. "I need to know everything you can tell me about the person who started the group."

"The who?"

The full weight of the hand gun came down on Sekane's face. "Not who? I need an answer. The leader, who is it? I need everything."

Sekane's eyes moved from side to side, aided with the strength of fear. He tried to come up with an answer, yet nothing came out of his mouth.

"Nothing to say? That's how we'll end it, then."

The figure moved in. He turned Sekane's body just slightly to the right before two quick puffs from the silencer made his body go limp. Sekane settled into the floor. The figure stood over him to admire what just happened. He put the gun back into the duffle. Sakane's eyes were frozen open in death. His mouth looked like he was about to speak.

He left him that way and moved quickly through the house, gathering the computer, checking for appointment books, notes on the desk, the cell phone, and any hiding spots for documents. There was still one important stop to make before sunrise.

He returned to the body.

The figure, still wearing gloves, adjusted the body so the area under the chin was exposed and easily available. There was a certain precision in the work, a practiced signature. A smile inched across the the figure's face as he pulled the ice pick from the bag.

6

Four minutes past Midnight, Jackie stood with her arms crossed, waiting for him to emerge from his car. "Butcher! I'm waitin' and I got to go inside." She turned briefly to see a light go out in the Never Too Late, then turned again to the subject in the car. She called to him again like she would urge a cat to come back inside. "Butcher..."

He was probably just two fingers above five-feet tall. Butcher got out of the all black BMW and walked toward Jackie. The biggest thing on him was the .45 sticking up out of his pants. "You need somethin' or you just taking a walk?" When he smiled, three scars could be seen on his left cheek.

"I don't need anything from you, but I need you to stay off my block."

Butcher stopped smiling. "This is a free country."

"Not here, it ain't. This is Jackie country and you will stay away from me, my people and anyone arriving at my door."

"Oh, you mean the special woman I saw this morning. She is free to talk to me."

"Butcher, the air is free but around here, that's about it. You're the drug man and I can't have you or that shit anywhere near my people."

"My, my, so rough. All I did was talk to her."

Jackie's eyes were as black as the night sky. Her brows like two crossed swords. The air was thick with Florida humidity, the birds no longer moving, nearby highway traffic was quiet. A soft wheezing came from the chest of Butcher, only to increase with intensity as Jackie took two strong steps toward him. She slowed her delivery to make sure he understood exactly what she was asking. "We both know you're not offering talk. What did she buy from you?"

"Why you so interested?" He studied her for a moment. "You and I got history."

Jackie uncrossed her arms. Both fists were now clenched in tight knots. The glare penetrated the thick air. "If you make one more run at people coming out of this center, I won't call police, I'll bust you up myself."

"And what, you'll call your son?"

Jackie almost made a move toward him but stopped.

Butcher seized on the moment. "You never called him before, like all those nights you left him for some sweetness." He drew in his breath like he was taking a hit off a pipe. "Or the night you left him with a friend and didn't come back for three days. I kept you supplied with the best stuff and you didn't seem to mind then."

"Those days are over. I made some mistakes. What you're doing now is keeping people down, just like you did with me. Now, what did you sell her?"

"Happiness." He started laughing until a wheeze cut it short.

He didn't see Jackie pick up the rock. The round missile whizzed by him and just missed his right cheek. "Hey, you know who you messn' with?" He placed a hand on the top of the gun.

"A fool," she yelled. Jackie picked up another rock. Jagged-edged nightmares ripped through her head. Butcher was part of her very own history of loving crack. Quick thoughts of burglaries, car-break-ins, and stolen purses moved through Jackie like kicks to the stomach. All of the actions led to pooling money to pay Butcher and the reward was the next high. And the loser was her son Frankie. The moments in time just made Jackie angrier. She found a larger rock and tossed the dirty sphere toward the car. The rock bounced off the hood, leaving a four-inch scratch.

Butcher started to pull the gun from his waist, then shoved it back. "I'm outta here, but this is not over. I don't know who that woman was, but she bought everything I had. My new best customer."

"And your last customer around here. Now, get the fuck out."

The BMW swallowed him up. Behind the wheel, he looked like a child driving a car. He tapped a middle finger on the glass window as he drove off.

7

Barry Ruddup started to slam the car door and instead closed it soft and tight. He stared hard at Kinnie. "Where's your purse?"

"What, you don't trust me?"

"No."

He grabbed the purse from her, rifling through the folds and zippered pockets. He fought off her attempts to get it back. "What's this?" He held up tiny bottles of vodka and one rum. He kept looking, finally pulling out five baggies, full of pills.

She grabbed at the air. "I need those. Get me through the night."

"Not tonight." He put them all down on the driveway, got back into his car and drove over the bottles and pills. The pop and crunch of each busted bottle pierced the early morning air.

"You'll get a flat tire."

"I don't care," he yelled. "You've cost us thousands of dollars. I'm spending all day mending the damage you caused." He studied her. "You got anything else?"

"You want me to strip? Cause I can do that." She started to pull on the bikini string top. He ran to her side. "No, don't do that."

Ruddup pointed the purse at her like it was a weapon. "The pills and vodka. Kinnie, c'mon, that combination will kill you."

"I'm doing fine."

"Fine! I pulled you from the ledge. This has to stop. Now."

"But I need them Barry." Kinnie Mason dropped her voice into the sultry, inviting deepness that had worked in the past. Ruddup always gave in to her wishes. "Just a couple of pills, Barry. Just a couple."

"Kinnie, what you need is to get off these things. Too much of them and one day, you'll never wake up."

She looked up and smiled at the sky of stars like they were diamonds sprinkled on crushed velvet. "The stars are like my pills. They make me happy. You want me to be happy, don't you, Barry?"

He tossed the purse at her. "I can't just look the other way. If you want to make me happy, let's finish the album. How about no more cancelled concerts. What about we finally do some new social media campaigns? There is a lot you can do to make me happy, but it has nothing to do with your damn pills."

A hint of a Florida breeze teased of cooler temps that would not come until later in the year. Maybe, she thought, just maybe, she could do one night without drugs.

He pointed to the front door of his house. The place was a one-story ranch style, with a long front facing the curb, a small fence guarding a wrap-around porch. Various croton plants stood at attention in front of the fencing. He took his time opening the door, unlocking two deadbolts before stepping into the foyer. Ruddup turned on the lights.

"Never been here before. Nice place." Mason looked over the dining space with the chair rails separating two shades of blue, top and bottom. "I like it," she smiled. There was a certain lackadaisical stride to her walk, still coasting from the mind-cruising blast of the opioids taken in the morning.

"Can I have a drink?" The question was followed by a howl of a laugh echoing off the imported leather couch, the sparkling quartz counter tops in the kitchen, and a line of paintings on the wall. "Just kidding."

"We need to talk." Ruddup locked up the door and made sure the shades were drawn.

"All this time, and you never invited me here." There was admiration in her face as she ran a finger on the couch. "Very nice. I pay you well."

On the wall, Mason saw three gold records in wood frames. The wall plaques represented years of work, time before the public and numerous interviews. Kinnie Mason took in a short breath. The records also reminded her of the lack of input on her part in the past year. The gold records should be replaced, she thought, by all the pills that have taken over her life. Just put the pills under glass and admire all the creativity they have snatched away. And yet, she knew, more than anything, that what she wanted right now, was another pill to swallow.

She also noticed the missing. On the walls and in the house, there were publicity photographs of her. Pictures with adoring fans and wide shots of performances. Yet, there was something missing. It took her a moment to figure it out. There were no pictures of Ruddup. Not with her, not with anyone. She looked out at the kitchen and tried to glance into the bedroom. No photographs anywhere. Before she could think on it more, the moment was replaced by the strong urge to ride a pill.

Ruddup spoke low and tried to sound convincing. "We have a session coming up. You were supposed to have four songs ready. I'm guessing you're not ready."

"Don't need any new songs."

Ruddup said, "What about earning a living? Meeting the requirements of the contract. We have a deadline for these songs, and what have you done?"

"Like I said, don't need any songs."

"Let's face it, you're a mess. And until you realize it, we're both going down."

"A mess huh?" She sat down in the plush touch of the couch. "I got my R's."

"R's? What's that?"

"My R's. My royalties."

"Sure, that's something but if you don't record, the public will forget about you."

"What, you afraid of not getting paid?"

"I hope you think more of me than just being your manager. I produce your concerts saving you a ton of money. I oversee your recordings, book your gigs, look after your fan mail, do the budget. I wear a lot of hats for you and in the end, you're saving."

She leaned her head against the couch and closed her eyes. "Right now, I just want to enjoy the fruits of my labor."

"By fruits, you mean getting high all day, every day. Drinking to the point of blacking out and standing naked on a hotel ledge. Is that what you mean?"

"I was okay."

"Look, it's late. Or I should say very early. Let's get some sleep. You take the back room. We'll talk about this in the morning."

Ruddup walked to the rear of the house and opened a door to a room with a bed covered in gold covers. "This is yours." She opened her eyes and walked into the room like a child being punished.

"Thanks."

"Just knock on my door if you need anything."

A few minutes after Ruddup retreated to his room, she stared down the hallway to make sure he was not coming back. She reached down and pulled open the top of the jeans and smiled. A four-inch pocket was sewn into the jeans. Mason pulled the zipper to reveal a stash of pills. He didn't crush all of them, she thought. Mason reached down and pulled out four pills. In the bathroom, she found a glass and filled it with water. She kept the swallows much quieter than her usual gulping, in case Ruddup checked on her one last time. Pills down, she walked back into the room. Now she wanted her space.

Kinnie opened the closet. Three pairs of shoes rested in the corner. Nothing else. She stepped inside and closed the door. This was exactly what she wanted. All darkness and let the pills take her on another journey.

Let it ride. Let it ride.

She wanted to feel every dying impulse, every energetic thought being clouded by the pills. Let her will and confidence shrivel with the night, blow-torch all positive thought and leave nothing for the mind to rebuild or even contemplate writing something so trivial as a song.

In the darkness, in the quiet, she heard something. She heard the noises again. Let it go, she thought, don't stop the journey. Ignore the noises.

The noises turned into the sounds of voices.

Kinnie opened the closet door. The sounds were louder now. She got up off the floor and stepped quietly to the bedroom door, opening just a few inches. She saw a large man, wearing gloves and something on his feet pulling Ruddup from the bedroom and into the family room. Mason squinted a few times. Was this real? Or part of her opiate-induced journey. She tried to push away the haze and get clear thoughts on what she was seeing. She opened the door even more and listened.

"But you already know why I'm here," the big man said.

"I did what I had to do. I had no choice. Either that..." Ruddup reached for a table leg, anything to stop being pulled. "You really made this difficult," the figure said. "I'm done talking."

"Wait!" Ruddup held up both hands.

"You gonna offer me money?" The man stood up and reached into his duffle. When the gun emerged with the long silencer, Kinnie dropped to the carpet floor. She pushed her hand across her mouth to squelch a yell.

Ruddup went limp as if resigned to what was about to happen next. He turned his eyes to the ceiling.

The figure got down close to Ruddup's head. "You knew this day was coming."

Ruddup turned his head, fixing his gaze on the rear bedroom and directly into the eyes of Kinnie Mason. Two puffs moved his head both times and Ruddup's body went still. His eyes open. The figure stared at Ruddup and followed the gaze until he was staring directly at her.

Face to face.

Mason slammed the door, clicked the lock and looked around the room for anything looking like a weapon. Seconds later, the boom against the door let her know he was trying to enter. She turned and reached the window when the door started to weaken from the heavy blows and the force on the other side of the wall.

The door smashed off the jamb. The figure looked around and found the room was empty. The window was open.

Kinnie Mason was running. Her lungs immediately ached from the severe lack of exercise in a life of music and pills. Everything in her body told her to stop. She saw a large patch of undeveloped land where more homes were about to be built in the area. For now, deep ruts on the sand and mud showed where big trucks were putting in the pipes for future bathrooms and kitchens. Infrastructure. She admonished Ruddup for being one of the first to buy, yet now she praised him. The cover was her only protection. She kept running.

Tentacles of pain reached every pore. Her heart rammed beats inside her chest. The headache was taking the top off her head. Each step pounded the grass and reverberated up through her legs and hips. Breathing was loud and forced.

A bullet cut into a low hanging palm frond. She never heard the shot. Two homes were on the right. A stop there might bring the figure with her and put others in danger. She kept going. A wide range of emotions tore through her. Why was Ruddup a target? What happened years ago? Who was the killer. The face was transfixed on her brain.

The face.

She fell. Just then she remembered her purse was still on the floor next to the bed. Her name and information was there for the killer. Her time on the ground was not long. Mason got up running. She ran like the next bullet was being lined up right now. Run like the time on earth was short, all used up and about to be cashed out.

Kinnie reached the main intersection. Instead of going to the convenience store on the corner, she hid in the bushes and waited. She gulped at the air, taking in as much as she could. Because she never wore a watch, all sense of time was off. Her only guess was six or seven minutes passed by. A car pulled into the store and a man got out.

The figure.

Her breathing had settled down. Kinnie's chest still racked with pain. She watched the man go inside the store and talk to the clerk. Even from where she was hiding, she could tell the conversation was about her. The figure described her height, showing the man his hand leveled off at about five-foot six. The clerk shook his head and the figure started to go back outside, then stopped just outside the door. She saw him stare up at the surveillance cameras.

The figure went back inside.

"No!" Kinnie Mason shouted.

She got up and began running toward the store. Maybe, she thought, maybe draw his attention off the cameras. Her running halted when she saw the clerk suddenly jerk from the shots, then slump over the counter. She was too late. The figure went to the back room. The snatching of the video card would only take a few seconds. A tear formed at her right eye. Mason withdrew to the thick trees and continued to wait.

The figure left.

Ninety minutes passed before she drew up the courage to walk inside the store, past the body somewhere on the floor and look for a telephone.

8

Jackie wrapped a blanket around a shivering Kinnie Mason. The right side of the bikini top was sliding down, and Jackie was looking around for something for her to wear. "It's eighty degrees outside and you're cold." Once Jackie found Kinnie, she drove to a nearby hotel lobby, and checked to make sure police were on the way.

Mason kept her eyes staring at an imaginary point in space, never blinking. "I have someone who will be here soon." Jackie kept looking at the door. A man entered.

"Kinnie, this is Frank Tower. He's a private investigator."

Frank Tower did not offer a hand, realizing the woman with the torn jeans probably would not reciprocate. Tower turned to Jackie. "Is Detective David on the way?"

"He'll be here any minute."

Tower wore a light zipper jacket, a way to keep his Glock out of sight. He leaned into Mason. "What she's not telling you is Jackie gave birth to me. She doesn't like to say I'm her son."

"Worst mother of the decade," Jackie whispered. "Told him not to call me mother."

Tower said, "She had me during her crack years and things didn't go too well. But that's over now."

"I loved crack more than him," Jackie delivered her confession to the wall, deciding not to directly address Mason.

Tower looked down the road, then back to Kinnie Mason. "When Detective David gets here, he will take over. I'm just looking out for the both of you until..."

The sun crested over a bank of gray-blue clouds.

A stout man with a crisp white shirt walked into the room followed by another man and two Stilton Bay police officers. "Morning Frank," Detective David shook hands with Tower and moved close to Mason.

"We're going to take this slow. I'm Mark. Mark David. With me, is Detective Sam Dustin. We were going to take you to the hospital."

"No! No hospital." Mason spoke for the first time since she was picked up on the road by Jackie. "Not safe. Not safe anywhere."

Detective David said, "Not safe? Who are you afraid of?" He looked down at his notes. "Did you know a Barry Ruddup?"

"Barry is, was my manager."

"Was anyone else home at the time?"

"No."

"Did you see?"

"Yes! I saw it. I saw that man kill Barry. Why Barry? He never hurt anyone."

"Did you get a good look at his face?"

"Yes," she said into the blanket. "The faces. I remember the faces. The faces!" She kept repeating the word "faces", yelling at the ceiling.

Jackie moved in and hugged her.

Detective David motioned to Tower to meet with him and Detective Dustin. They walked into the hallway. David turned to Tower. "We've got a problem."

"You sure you want him to hear all this?" Dustin took his finger and jammed it into Tower's chest. Tower took the finger and started to roll the digit over and take him down. David stopped Tower. The two stood apart, glaring at each other. David spoke first, "I decide what we release and who gets the information."

Dustin was not finished. "So, a washed-up cop, let me change that, possibly a dirty cop who stole money, gets the inside on this investigation?"

Tower countered. "I was cleared, and I left, you know that."

Dustin spat at the ground. "The case is still open. Your name could come up again."

Mark David spoke up. "This, investigation, as you put it, is not ours."

Tower was confused. "This is not Stilton Bay's case?"

"No." Mark David pulled Tower to the side. "We've got a problem. A big problem." His voice dropped to a need-to-hear-only tone. "The man she saw. The man in the house with Barry Ruddup is a contract man."

Tower said, "Who is Barry Ruddup?"

"Ruddup was Mason Kinnie's manager."

"I'm familiar with her songs. She's good."

"Well, Ruddup was killed early this morning. Two to the back of the head. With a calling card."

Tower looked back at Jackie giving a cup of water to Mason. "A calling card?"

"Ya see, Ruddup has been with her for the past nine years. But Ruddup is not his real name." David again referred to his notes. "His name was Marcus Tinson."

"I think I remember the name."

"Tinson testified at a big trial almost thirteen years ago. He was in witness protection."

"Was?"

"Correct. He left witness protection on his own accord six months into the program. Let me be clear about this, witness protection is just fine. There are no problems there. This guy went rogue. Decided he could do things his own way. He just probably did not figure this way."

"Wow. That's an old case."

"There are a couple of problems. Ruddup wasn't the only hit."

In the five years Tower was on the force, each new case of bad news, a new murder case, another act of leaving a child alone, a domestic violence shooting, all of them had a way of hardening Tower, to the point that fresh facts never made him flinch anymore. He took in the information, looking directly into the staid green eyes of Detective Mark David.

"What are we talking about?" Tower said.

"Including Ruddup, we have three hits. Three hits in two days." David said. "All three men decided to leave witness protection years ago."

"All three testified in trial?" Tower asked.

"Bingo. Big cases. All different, but the result was the same. A lot of people went to prison."

Dustin spoke up. "What I don't understand is why he moved so fast. Three in two days?"

Tower answered his question. "Because he knows after the first hit, we'll be contacting all other former witnesses. He had to move on as many people as possible."

"And he left a calling card," David continued. "Each man had an ice pick jammed up through the bottom of his mouth, up and into the brain." David gave the account flatly, like he was ordering a large pizza with extra cheese. "The killer was saying 'I'm going to close your mouth forever.'"

"The ice picks were left at the scene?" Tower was thinking through the facts.

"Yes," David said. "Even though he chased our survivor, looks like he went back to jam the ice pick into Ruddup." David rubbed fingers through his hair. "What do you know about her?" He looked back through the hallway at Kinnie Mason.

Tower said, "Jackie didn't want to say much since she is a client, but she's a user. Dependent on opioids, alcohol, PCP. Just about anything she can get. She needs help."

"That's great," Dustin said. "Our one and only witness to see this guy and she's an addict."

David took his gaze from Mason. "I'm hoping she can work with our sketch artist. We need to move on this fast. The feds are taking over. They won't be here for a couple of days."

Tower looked at them. "Okay, then I'm on my way."

"That's just it. You can't go yet. We need your help."

9

"Sublingual gland." Chief crime technician Donald Crespo was repeating the words for a second time as Detective Mark David wrote notes. "It's the gland just under the tongue."

"I get it," David said.

"The ice pick went up through that gland, through the tongue and into the brain cavity. Not pretty."

Barry Ruddup's body was still in the same place. The house was surrounded by uniforms checking the grounds, looking for a piece of clothing, a dropped gun, anything. Crespo's slow moves were holding up the body removers. "Just give me a minute," he told them. "My way of thinking, the pick was the guy's way of shutting him up, closing his mouth, so to speak."

Crespo did his business as detectives watched him. He turned the body over, only after a lengthy search of the body and anything close-by. He treated the scene as a circle, and worked his way in, toward the victim. He didn't want to step on a drop of blood. Patience was the best policy.

"Any residuals?" David looked up from his notepad.

"DNA? Not yet. Too early. From what we could see in the bedroom, the prints in the carpet were very flat, like he was wearing something over his shoes. I do have a theory."

"Go ahead."

"Well," Crespo used the top of his wrist to scratch his nose, rather than use his bloody plastic gloves. "We know he got in through the back door and must have surprised Ruddup here. But there is also evidence, no prints I'm afraid, that he turned the door knob to the main bedroom, probably looking to see if anyone was in there, before making his attack."

"And she was in the back bedroom."

"Then she just missed the first direct confrontation."

David said, "That would come later."

"Ruddup took two in the back of the head. Up close and clean. She saw that." He paused. "What are you thinking."

"My old partner thinks we better move fast."

"Frank Tower?"

"Yeah." David motioned to the two waiting men to put Ruddup in a body bag and take him to the morgue. "Tower thinks this guy is going from a list."

"A list?"

"Yeah. Makes sense. He thinks he is going down a list and hitting as fast as he can. And for us, we have to move just as fast."

"And she saw his face..."

David thought about Kinnie Mason. "And this guy knows that. She will, I'm sure, be his biggest priority. He might even stop moving on the list until he takes her out."

"Aren't the feds coming?"

"Sure, but I'm not going to wait until we get a call on another body. My guess is others are due to meet him. Maybe soon."

"All former witness protection?"

"Looks that way. And why not Florida? Sun, the water."

"Mark, this guy is a pro. Took the computer, Ruddup's cell phone, the girl says he used a silencer."

David put down his notepad. "Does it look like he brushed up against anything?"

"So far, no. In one house, he came in through the sky light. Dropped down from the ceiling. In another, he also came in through the back. In all three, the computers were taken."

"We have to get to the next victim before he does."

10

Shannon Tower waited until her husband was almost finished packing before she spoke. "So, when will I see you?" She had tension in her voice, yet there was a certain comfort in her brown eyes, a look that Tower first noticed about her, like an invitation to sit and talk. She came up to his chest in height, kept her hair long, never changing the look since the day they met. When she did not hear a response, asked again, "When?"

"Should be just a few days." Frank Tower stuffed two more shirts into a roller luggage bag. "The feds will take over. I'm doing a favor for Mark."

"It's not every woman who takes back her husband after he has an affair."

Frank Tower stopped what he was doing and embraced the slender-framed Shannon. "When this is over, I will make this up to you. Please know, I love you." He closed the bag and eased it to the floor.

Shannon had a habit of adjusting her hair as she talked. The more she wanted to make a point, the more she pulled at the strands of her dark hair. She had a routine of wearing something lavender during the week. Reds on Friday.

She said, "You were short on the phone. What is this about? I haven't heard anything on the news."

"They told the media these were possible suicides. They are not. A hit man is targeting people who left witness protection. I'm helping guard the main witness. Jackie is involved."

"Jackie?"

"This witness has a problem. All of us will be staying somewhere."

Shannon stood there, absorbing what she had just heard. She went over to a table, opened a drawer, and pulled out a small stack of brochures. "I was going to ask you about something." She waved the stack at Tower.

"What is this, a vacation?"

"No. Our future. Away from Stilton Bay. A new direction for us. These are cities."

"A new place? We're settled here."

"I know. I just think since we are back together again, we need a fresh start somewhere else. I've been making phone calls."

Trust. The word was now looming large in their relationship. Tower winced as the thoughts pushed to the back of his memories were now a center-piece. He couldn't avoid what he did. The affair with a client almost toppled the marriage. Shannon refused to talk to him for months. Jackie became the go-between and eventually got them talking again. Even now, driving down the street, Tower shakes his head, wondering what was he thinking? The matters became complicated when the so-called other woman was murdered. Tower stared at Shannon. He didn't know how to proceed. He wanted to stay in Stilton Bay, yet he didn't want to upset Shannon. For now, he decided to keep listening.

Shannon flipped the very end of one curl over and over in her fingers. "Frank, I really want you to think about it. Stilton Bay is nice, but you can open your office in another state."

"It's not that easy."

Shannon moved closer to him. "Please, just give it some thought. We can talk when you get back."

"You can text me, but no phone calls unless it's an emergency. Is that okay?"

Shannon smiled and gave the curl one good tug.

11

Kinnie Mason waited until no one was watching and tugged on her jeans until she could see her stash hidden in an inner pocket. Seven pills left. Worry dug into two lines above her eyes. Normally twelve to fifteen pills got her through a day. *Maybe I can spread them out.* She closed the jeans before Jackie walked back into the room.

Jackie was carrying a bowl of fruit. Bananas and cut strawberries with a few blueberries. "Got to eat, girl. And I don't mean fast food. You need this." Blinking from a lack of sleep, she placed the bowl in front of Kinnie, who looked like she was being forced to eat worms. Her stomach tightened.

Jackie took her face with her right hand, forcing Kinnie to look directly at her. "Look, you and I both know what's about to happen. You're in police custody for your own protection. That means you are about to go into withdrawal. I can help you with that."

She had direct attention, so Jackie took her hand down. "It's going to take several days, more or less. I can help you each step of the way. I've been through it myself. Three times."

"Kept going back?"

Jackie's voice softened. "My Frankie was four when I left him. No sitter. Nobody. I thought I would be gone one hour. I left him a bit of food, but I didn't come back till the next day. I had to have my crack. When I came home, his pants were off, piss and poop everywhere, like a puppy. He was crying and had a cut on his head. The kid was starving. And you know what

I was thinking about? How fast I could clean him up so I could go back out there and score more crack. Girl, I was a mess."

"Does he remember anything?"

"Frankie? I don't think so. But that was the first time I went into withdrawal. Not gonna lie. It was terrible." Jackie grabbed a nearby pillow like she was holding a baby. "Did it for my Frankie."

"It didn't last?"

"Naw. My friends got me hooked again. Sorry asses." Jackie looked at the bowl. "Eat something."

"I'm not real hungry."

Jackie's eyes closed and opened and sleep was winning the battle. "The sketch artist will be here soon. You've got to start eating better."

"I just need to go to the bathroom."

Jackie watched as Kinnie walked away and closed the door. Then Jackie shut her eyes. Locked in sleep, she did not move. The world she provided for Kinnie consisted of three officers outside the door, all cell phone usage stopped, hotel phone shut down, and orders to stay inside. No walks outside. Jackie felt like she was in jail, a place familiar to her with four arrests on her sheet, all for panhandling, trespassing and one burglary count. No prostitution.

Inside the bathroom, Kinnie was at war with herself. Go into withdrawal now, or keep up with the pills. She didn't bother answering the question. The pills had control of her body. She looked down into the secret pocket sewn in her jeans. Kinnie took out two of the pills and swallowed them down with a strong sip from the faucet. She had a craving for something stronger but settled for the tap water. Kinnie sat on the toilet, closed her eyes and arched backward until she had a place to rest her head.

Damn, she thought. I want some PCP. And a tall glass of vodka would do just nicely. She let her mind drift off to somewhere else. She became warm and removed the dirt-laden bikini top. Her breasts swelled with the false confidence the drugs provided. She shook off the jeans, then the panties, and eased down into the empty tub. Just get naked, Kinnie thought, and coast with the pills. Queen Mason was back.

Let it ride, let it ride.

A few words of a new song permeated the clouded thinking. Then, the words went away, shrouded in the haze of a charcoal mist. Mason opened the bathroom door and walked into the middle of the room hoping for, then soon realizing, there wasn't a bottle of vodka to go with the high. She looked out the window. The burst of morning sunlight caught the shuttered eyes of Jackie and she woke up. "What the!" Jackie stood up and stared into the pinhole-sized pupils of Kinnie Mason. "Where's your clothes?" Jackie rushed into the bathroom, retrieved the clothing and lashed the bikini top around a bare chest. "I see your eyes. Where did you get it?" Jackie's voice was calm and direct. "Where did you get your stuff?"

When Mason did not speak, Jackie called for a female police officer into the room. When the straight-shouldered form of a female uniform appeared, Jackie gave the orders. "Pat her down."

Less than ten seconds into the search, the officer found the stash pocket in the jeans and pulled out the pills.

"No!" Mason was flailing her arms, kicking at the officer, and shouting "no!" over and over. Finally, she tried to stand apart from them both, yelling she wanted her freedom. They just let her stand there, kicking at the open air. Her hair draped all around her face, missing her intended targets by several feet.

"What's going on?" Frank Tower arrived. He stared at Jackie and the officer. "The sketch artist is here with her laptop."

Jackie pointed to Mason. "Our witness is not ready yet."

12

Three separate fire hoses crisscrossed the highway, all meeting at the ball of flames in the center of the road. Fire fighters hit the blaze with continued blasts of water. A twenty-foot column of black smoke curled into the air. People stood on the sides of the road, even parking so they could get a good look.

"They tell me someone is cooking a car." Detective Mark David stared into the mass of flames.

Gil Mako took his gaze away from his crew. Stilton Bay Fire was emblazoned on his helmet. "Yeah, I'm the one who called you out. Thought you might be interested."

"Okay. Whatcha got?"

"I've been reading your internal memos. Yeah, the fire department smoke eaters read them too. The car looks a lot like the one you described. Possibly belonged to one of your victims."

David stepped about twelve paces closer to the smoked car. "You sure? I can't even make out the model."

"Two-door. Tan to beige color. All black wheels."

"That's it." David moved closer, so close, he started to choke. "Yeah, now I see it. Or what's left of it." He turned to Mako. "You find anything inside?"

"Not yet. Too hot. We did a check. No bodies and nothing in the trunk. We're trying to get the VIN numbers."

The overhead smoke was turning white, a clear sign the fire fighters were winning. Two hoses where shut down. The remaining water line kept up a water assault on the two-door. David and Mako looked inside. "Not much here," Mako said.

David pulled up a report on his cell phone. "I've got a county-wide alert on a stolen car just outside the city. That's a one-mile walk from here."

"What are you thinking?" Mako wiped a line of sweat inside his helmet.

"This car was heading north, out of the city. The stolen car was also seen moving north. Maybe our hitter is leaving us." David took out his notepad. "Any plates?"

"We didn't find any." Mako was walking around the car.

"I'm guessing this guy wiped it down first and then got the flames going." David looked around. "I don't see any surveillance cameras around."

"This guy picked the one spot that's a dead zone." Mako watched as the last hose was turned off. "It's all yours. We were gonna call a wrecker, but I'm assuming..."

"Correct. We'll take it off your hands." David's cell blasted out a ring. "Mark David."

"You got a minute? I'm here at the morgue." Donald Crespo's voice sounded winded.

"I've got time. What's up?" David started walking to his car.

"I need you over here pronto. You have to see this. And bring Frank Tower."

"Tower?"

"Bring him."

13

Frank Tower followed the directions of the desk clerk and walked the long corridor toward the big doors. This was not Tower's first time to the morgue. The homicide unit, thinking Tower would be next-in-line for a detective slot, often asked him to observe while he was on the force. Never fainting, he stood firm through autopsies of a knife victim, three car crashes, a shotgun death and a sixth-floor jumper. All the while, he thought at one time he might see Jackie on the metal table, a victim of the demon drugs.

"What is he doing here?" Sam Dustin's face contorted into a disjointed mash of cheek movements, punctuated by five-day beard stubble. He looked at Tower as if he wanted to spit somewhere on the newly polished white tile.

"He was told to be here." Mark David stuck his pad into the side of his pants. "Crespo wanted to see him."

"He's not city."

"I know, but he was a uniform for seven years."

"I remember." The ends of Dustin's smile pulled back, revealing teeth as white as the floor. "Didn't end well."

"Let's get this over with." Tower stood off to the side, waiting for more instructions.

Donald Crespo pushed the doors open with his shoulder, leaving his plastic gloves free from contact. "C'mon gentlemen. Sorry to keep you waiting." The doors were just the beginning of a series of more doors and a turn to the left before entering the morgue itself.

Old thoughts cascaded through Tower. He was used to the smell of the place, yet circumstances haunted him. This was the very place, two years earlier, where Tower was escorted to identify the body of his mistress. A murder with all the clues linking Tower, however, an alibi gave Tower enough weight to remove him as a suspect. An alibi provided by the one person who knew exactly where Tower was at the time of the murder. Shannon, his wife. A chill rifled down Tower's back, remembering the conversation convincing Shannon to testify and clear Tower for the murder of the woman who cheated with her husband. Shannon could have claimed a memory loss and Tower might be residing today in the Florida penitentiary. Instead, Tower was prepared to help Mark David find the killer.

Tower looked around the morgue and shook off the grim reminders. There were no bodies in view. Before them, Crespo had arranged three ice picks. Each pick was on a table, with a name plate off to the side. "What we have here gentlemen, are the ice picks found on our three victims." He turned to Tower. "The reason I asked you here is because, I think you had a case of the same knife being used in a series of cases some years ago?"

Tower was still adjusting to the coldness of the room. "Yes, we had two cases, then a third case two years later. The same type of knife."

"Did they catch the killer?" Crespo was walking toward the picks as he spoke.

"No."

"But, there was a message on them?"

"Just some initials carved into the knife."

"Okay. Gentlemen, take a look at these picks and tell me if you see anything. And no, I didn't find any prints."

Dustin, Mark David and Tower all leaned down, getting as close to the ice picks as possible without touching them. Dustin was the first to speak. "I see a pattern, but I don't see anything." He stepped back.

David came second. "Looks like a bunch of nothing."

Crespo picked up one of the ice picks with a gloved hand. "That's what I thought. But my gut feeling tells me something is here. I wanted everyone here in case I missed something."

Tower was still examining the pick. "You put them under a microscope?"

"Yes. Intersecting lines, but no real message. Before I gave up, I wanted to ask the three of you to look."

"What about an impression." Tower pointed to the pick closest to him. "If you take a close look, you can see the end sticks out a bit."

"Okay. Let me try that." The three waited until Crespo made the solution for a mold pour. He mixed the brew and stuck each ice pick into the batch. Within a few minutes of cooling, he pulled off the mold. Then, he used a different solution to pour into the impression. Another ten minutes went by. Dustin looked weary. David took out his pad. Tower just watched. Crespo took the finished product and stuck the form into a small vat of ink. He pressed the mold form onto a piece of paper. He stood back.

"Shit," Dustin shouted.

"Gentlemen, I think Mr. Tower gets a gold star."

On the paper, in a clear, distinct imprint, all four men could easily see the words three/seven.

Tower said, "To me, that means three of seven. That can only mean this was the third person on his list of seven."

"Exactly." Crespo was already preparing the remaining two ice picks for immersion into the ink. Several minutes later, he had three sheets of paper. All with an impression. Four of seven and five of seven.

"Who is five of seven?" David asked.

"Ruddup is my guess," Tower answered.

"You're right." Crespo was lining up the three impressions for a photograph. "Barry Ruddup was victim, or hit, number five."

Tower's eyes revealed he was in deep thought. "If Ruddup was the last victim, that means there are two more on his list. Two victims, or marks, to go."

David looked up from his notes. "And there are two other victims, already dead, that we don't know about. We have some work to do."

Dustin's face turned dour. He rested his hands on his hips. Mark David took notice. "What's up?"

Dustin pointed to Tower. "What's up is he's here. If this ever goes to trial, some smart lawyer is going to eat us up 'cause we brought Tower into the case. Chain of command with the evidence."

Crespo pointed to himself. "I brought him here. Me. He is an outside consultant. And I will testify to that. I trust Frank's judgement. You have a problem with that, step out of the room."

Silence.

Tower got ready to leave as Mark David updated his notes.

14

"Can I speak to you for a minute?" Jackie pulled Mark David into the hallway. "She's very fragile right now."

"Did she finish with the sketch artist?"

"Yes, but there are some complications." Jackie glanced into the room as if to make sure Mason was not watching. "She is about to go into withdrawal. And that won't be pretty. Right now, her normal day is to start with vodka, move to the pills, then start the whole process over again in several hours. You need her. And you need her happy. The only way for that to happen right now is to let her keep using. And Mark David, I'm not going to stand by and watch that." She made a soft stomp with her right foot. "Do you understand?" The words came through her gritted teeth.

"How much time do we have?"

"Like now."

"What do you want me to do?"

"You have to convince her to go into rehab, right away, or she's going to revolt."

Mark David absorbed the words. He let his hand rest on his chin. "Do you think she understands this?"

Jackie pinched her fingers. "Not really. She's about this close to feeling sick. The only thing she knows is her body needs the pills to survive. Get your witness into rehab."

"I have to make some calls."

"You do that. And fast."

They both went back to the hotel room.

Mason studied the artist's computer version of the killer and she looked at the assembled detectives like a child needing approval on a new crayon drawing.

"You did good," Jackie said.

"Thank you. I'm ready to go home now." Mason turned her attention to the window and the glistening blue hotel pool down below.

Jackie was still examining the sketch. "They can't let you go just yet. He's still out there somewhere. For your own safety, we want to keep you here."

Mason looked at the semi-circle of Sam Dustin, Mark David, Frank Tower, Jackie and in the hallway, two uniforms. "I've been here for a day now. Anyway, can I get some fresh air?"

Another thoughtful look on Mark David's face was followed by an answer. "We can arrange that." He walked off and talked to the uniforms. Jackie turned to them, pulled out her cell phone, and made a phone call. Dustin pulled Frank Tower aside, marching him out the door, stopping at the ice maker. "You know you shouldn't be here." Dustin did not give Tower a chance to respond. "Someone is going to question why a civilian is part of the investigation and that could really screw things up."

Tower said, "Again, I was invited here."

"I know. But that doesn't make it right."

Tower turned to David, and then back to Dustin. "As soon as anyone tells me to leave, I'm outta here."

A loud siren and flashing lights filled the hallway with noise and confusion. A recorded voice was heard on all the speakers in the building.

"Please get out of the building. We have a general fire alarm. Please get out of the building, the fire department is on the way."

The uniforms were caught in the rush of two couples hurrying from their room. Another family emerged with two small children.

Kinnie Mason stared at the fire alarm she had just pulled and positioned herself by the door.

Mark David entered the room. "We've got to get out of here. Now." He turned and surveyed the rooms. "Where's Kinnie?" he yelled.

Tower and Dustin searched closets and each room. Nothing. Jackie searched the hallway. "There," she shouted.

Tower caught a glimpse of a pink bikini top disappearing into the stairway entrance. He gave chase. Dustin was right behind him. When he reached the stairs, Tower was taking them three at a time, jumping down to the next landing, echoes of his shoes bouncing off the walls. Tower made it down three flights and saw no sign of Mason. He stopped and listened. Hearing no sounds, he backtracked. "Maybe she got off on a floor," Tower shouted to Dustin.

"I'll get off this floor. You keep going downstairs." Dustin shoulder-smashed the door open and left Tower. Four minutes later Tower pushed through the doors and out onto the street. Jackie was already there.

"I took the elevator," she said.

Tower looked in all directions. No Kinnie Mason. A minute later, he was joined by Dustin. The three of them searched the car lot, the gift shop and the lobby. Still nothing.

They ran out into the street, checking cabs, sidewalks and the few restaurants near the hotel. After a brief run through side-streets, they all converged back in front of the hotel.

Jackie said, "She made her decision."

Tower was winded. "Decision?"

"Either the drugs or police protection. And she chose the drugs."

15

Kinnie Mason made the cab driver park a block away from her house. Seeing a police car outside, she hid in the neighbor's plush landscaping while figuring out a plan. "Move dammit," she whispered. Mason stayed low, walking past a row of hibiscus hedges and a spray of yellow-red croton plants. She stopped when she reached the back of her property, all the while making sure her neighbor did not mistake her for a burglar.

When she was well out of view, Mason ran for the rear door. She made a break past the pool, a row of patio chairs and the connected spa. The creeps, as she called them, were calling. Mason felt the urge in her body that something was missing. An extra ingredient she needed in order to function.

Her pills.

Inside, she stayed away from the windows. The police car was still out front, probably on the watch for her showing up. She crept upstairs to the seven bedrooms. Hers was the second on the right. Mason had a thing for making everything gray. The bed sheets, cover, drapes, carpet, bathroom tile and the wall paint, were all various shades of gray.

She closed the door to the bedroom and smiled. Mason had a compartment built into the bed frame. The covering even had bedding material over the outside, so no one noticed. Not even Barry Ruddup. The smile evaporated at the thought of seeing him killed. She reached down and opened the small door. Inside, there were plastic bottles of everything she needed.

"Yes!" she shouted at the walls. She cradled the bottles like finding a lost one-hundred-dollar bill. One plastic bottle dropped, and she caught it in mid-air. Kinnie Mason kissed the top of each bottle, rolling her eyes to the ceiling and letting a warm shudder go through her body as though she was in the midst of a double orgasm. Who needed a man? All she ever wanted or cared about rested in her hands, ready to be swallowed. There was no reason to return to a studio, practice her voice or write the next damn song. Who needed that?

She picked the right pills and poured out six into her hand. Before she took them, she noticed the lights of a police car turn on. Then the siren pierced the air. The car took off down the street. More pressing matters, she thought. No need to have police stay in front of Kinnie Mason's door.

One more pill, she thought. In her hurry to suck in the pill, the thing dropped to the ground, getting lost in the carpet.

Pills down, she turned on the music and listened to her last CD. She needed one more thing. Vodka! Kinnie pulled on the other drawer and saw her prize. With the cap off, she downed the clear liquid, letting some of it roll down her cheeks like tears. Only she wasn't crying.

Not now.

The ceiling was covered in speakers. They were located in certain locations throughout the house, all ready to blast at the touch of Kinnie's finger. Just ride the music. She stayed in that position, head swimming to the effect of the drugs and coasting on a guitar riff.

Yet still, she was able to hear a noise coming from somewhere downstairs. Mason got up, turned off the music and stood waiting for another sound.

She approached the stairs, ears strained to hear anything. Convinced there was something, she placed her bare foot on the step. Then another. As she stepped downward, more of the room came into view. Mason's head bounced from one side of the room to the other. Her breathing increased. A thumping deep inside her breast pounded.

Now in the living room, a quick scan of the space provided no answers.

Three more steps took her close to the French doors. "Ouch!" She looked down and noticed a small red dot on her right foot. A trickle of blood formed near the source of the pain. Mason picked at the foot and pulled out a small piece of glass. She examined the clear jagged nugget like it was a fresh made diamond. Her eyes searched the room for other pieces of broken glass. Hobbling, she made it to a kitchen drawer and pulled out a bandage. Thoughts moved through her pill-induced mind. Where did the glass come from? Where did the noise come from?

Maybe, she reasoned, there was nothing. Mason rubbed the sore foot and turned toward the stairs.

Then she stopped.

Deep within her, Mason called upon the primitive senses given to all of us. Vast studies have been done on the body's ability to perceive a stare or someone sneaking up on them. She did not want to turn around, yet she felt the strong pull of emotion that someone was close and watching her movements. She stood there, eyeing the stairs and weighing other options. Next came the voice.

"Hello, Kinnie. I've been waiting for you."

16

Without another thought, Mason dove for the floor. Her first impulse was to dodge the bullets she knew would be coming in her direction. She tasted the floor cleaner her maid used on the tile. Mason waited for the voice. When nothing came, she ran for the French doors, turning the knob and smashing through them at the same time, never looking back, always running. She kept going until she crashed into a figure moving at her from the right side.

It was him.

"You okay?" Frank Tower tried to straighten her up.

"No!" She tried to speak, only to give in to the lack of exercise and agility. Her lungs burned from the quick run. She tried to speak while gasping for air. The words were like crushed clouds, barely there. "He's in there."

"What? Speak up. Who?"

"He's in there. In the kitchen."

"Stay here." He pulled out his cell phone and tossed it to Mason. "Call 9-1-1." Tower pulled out his Glock and moved around the house to the open doors. The Glock was up, in both hands, classic police procedure. He gave the kitchen a side-to-side check. He gave judgement on the room as heavy and light. Any possible threat area was considered heavy. He saw no movement and went inside, gun up and ready. He stared down a long hallway. Nothing. One by one, Tower cleared the lower floor. He was just about to go upstairs, when he heard a familiar voice.

"Tower!" Detective Dustin held a gun aimed at Tower's side. "I'll take it from here. Back seat. Outside."

Tower moved back out to the front of the house. Seven police cars were now taking up the entire block. Three more cars were arriving. Overhead, a police helicopter did a large circle over the area. Two uniforms with police dogs searched the back yard. Down the block, another uniform shut down the street, not letting anyone pass and stretched a line of yellow crime tape across the road.

Tower stood next to Mason.

"Did you get him? Is he still there?"

"They're checking." Tower started to put an arm around her to give comfort, then drew back.

Mason said, "How did you know I was here?"

"You came back for the drugs, didn't you?"

There was a long pause and no answer. She waved off the paramedics. "Is that what you think?"

"As long as you keep lying, the worse it's going to stay. You must have a stash up there." Tower stared at the second floor. "You know the hotel wanted to press charges once they found out someone pulled the fire alarm. That is, until they were told it was you. Then they backed off. Gave you a pass." He got up close, staring directly into her pinhole sized pupils. "Remember, he stole your purse. Your address was in there. He's probably been waiting here, just sticking around to see if you came back. And you did."

"He spoke to me."

"Make sure you tell the detective."

"He said, 'I've been waiting for you.' I thought of Barry all over again."

Detective Mark David approached.

He was seething. "You evacuated a hotel, leaving police protection, just so you could run back here and do drugs?" Before she had a chance to respond, he kept going. "Yeah, we found your stuff. Nice hiding place."

"You get him?" Kinnie looked down at the ground.

Mark David glared at her. "Top to bottom. No one in there."

She told him what she heard. He was still upset. "Here's the deal." His voice was calmer now. "We're a small department. We don't have the people to watch you round the clock. We can't hold you; you're not a suspect. You're a witness. Technically, you are free to go. I advise you right now to stay with a friend. Stay away from this place. Keep in touch with us and please, get some help."

He walked away.

Enter Dustin. "Tower, your advising days are over."

"You're here because I played out my hunch."

"Like your hunch and the missing seventy- grand."

"I was cleared of that years ago."

Dustin got up in his face. "You still fucking your clients?"

Tower said, "I had one..."

"One what? Affair, tryst, Midnight titty run? What would you call it?"

"She came on to me."

"That's the story you're telling? Weak, Tower, real weak. You didn't belong on the force, and you don't belong on my crime scene."

Tower's right hand balled into a tight fist.

"Go ahead Tower. Punch me out in front of all these witnesses. Go for it."

Tower stepped back. Dustin disappeared behind the fire rescue truck.

Kinnie Mason looked at her home through sore eyes. She wanted to cry but nothing came. She turned to Frank Tower.

"I want to hire you."

17

"This is going to be short." Mark David stood at the front of the room. Up on a white board was the sketch based on the information from Kinnie Mason. There was nothing distinctive about the computer drawing. Nothing stood out. A thousand guys could look like that. The sketch was hard to tell if he was even black or white.

"He was spotted this morning at the home of the witness," David continued. The room was packed with officers, Highway Patrol, even the bomb squad. "We thought he was heading out of town; however, that proved to be wrong. He must have doubled back. What we know is that we have information on the three victims so far. I say so far, because we believe there might be two more victims very soon. We have cooperation from every facet of all agencies and we are trying to narrow down a list of targets, from people who left various witness protection programs on their own. We have a separate team working on that. What we need is for everyone to put some eyes on this guy. Right now. Before he makes another move."

David walked to a screen just above his desk. "We know that before Florida, there were two other victims. Dustin has that information."

Detective Dustin picked up two folders off his desk. He opened the first, taking a hard look at them like a man trying to decide if he needed reading glasses or not. "It took an extensive computer search to match an M.O. but we came up with two hits just like the ones here. A forty-eight-year old man living in central Illinois was shot two years ago. And two weeks later, in Tennessee, another victim. Sixty years old. Both victims were shot and jammed with an ice pick. Before you ask, yes, both had testified in respective trials. In one, the defendant skimmed from a bank. In the other, it was another Ponzi scheme. And both dropped out of sight rather than any type of witness protection. Somehow, our guy found out about them. I am handing out a cheat-sheet on both cases. You'll get them as you leave."

Dustin looked down a long sheet of notes. He raised his finger, indicating he had something to add. "The first victim, the forty-eight-year old. We found a picture of him in his house, with wounds and everything, except, we never recovered his body. It's missing."

David took over. "We don't have much time. It looks like our killer has been planning this for a long time. How he finds them is on our to-do list. What concerns me right now is the next two victims. We know he is targeting seven people. We believe there are five dead. So now, we have to reach the others. We have people tracking them down. The problem is the people who testified went underground. On their own. No forwarding information to anyone. Not even law enforcement. That makes it tough. The list is not long, but we need to get to them first. And right now." David paused. "Now, go get him."

18

All the bouys and markers made it easy to put the boat into position, just like angling for a soft kiss. "Ya did good." Kernan Bonson pulled on his well-developed beard and stared into the deck area of the boat and yelled. "T.K., where are ya?" Bonson pulled all the lines tight and waited. A full minute went by and he bellowed into the salted air of the Atlantic. "T.K. I know you're on the boat. This rig didn't park by itself! Now, where you be?"

Still no answer. Bonson pulled on the beard that hasn't seen a cutting in thirty-seven years. "If you can hear me, T.K. I got your order in the store. Provisions and a case of your favorite booze. All waitin' for ya."

Bonson turned around and found himself staring into the face of T.K. "Good Lordy, how did you do that? I never saw you move off that boat."

"I move fast." T.K.'s chin and face were chaffed, like someone had taken sandpaper to his skin. He was not the tallest or the biggest. He kept his brown eyes behind the sunglasses. "I won't be here long. Just long enough to load up."

"Where ya headed this time?" Bonson made it his mission to keep an eye on T.K.'s movements.

T.K. removed his sunglasses. "You know I never say where I'm going." He put the glasses back in place. "Now, where is my booze?"

They both walked off toward the dock store. Neither of them heard or felt the steps of another man walking with purpose on the dock and hiding behind any structure he could find.

There was no one else inside the store. The marina had the pristine presence of a painting. The smaller boats dipped politely in the calm wake, masts tinkling from the riggings. The melodic cadence of the swaying masts was almost hypnotic. The place was peaceful.

"Anyone been in asking about me?" T.K. stared into the eyes of Bonson.

"Naw. No one."

"You sure?"

"Yep. Don't see you here unless it's somethin' important."

"Maybe."

"C'mon, T.K."

"Thanks." T.K. took out a bottle. He studied the label and was tempted to open the sucker right there. When he looked back at Bonson, he was blank-faced, like someone had just unplugged him from the circuitry of the world. T.K. dropped immediately to the floor. He looked back at Bonson. The man stood there transfixed. Then, he fell forward. The hard noise made a dozen seagulls scatter. The back of Bonson's head had a small red smear. Blood dripped onto the wooden floor. T.K. tried to remember if Bonson had a gun in the store. He crawled toward the counter, making as little sound as possible. There had to be a weapon near the cash drawer, he thought. The crawl was slow. He kept listening for the gunman.

T.K. tried to gauge the distance and placement of the shooter. In a quick second, he went over all the details leading up to the shot. He did not hear any glass break. There was no sound of a door opening. He looked up. No mirror or surveillance cameras and still no one around. T.K. worked himself to the base of where the cash drawer was located. The next move would be tricky. He stood up in a slow movement, never intending to stand erect, just halfway and always behind cover. His hands reached into a shelf just below the counter. He rummaged through paper, scattered paperclips, a box of large fishing hooks and a writing pen. No gun. He dared a glance at the door.

"You can't escape." The voice came from the cooler. Bonson kept the thing stacked and packed with bags of ice.

T.K. looked around the room. "What is this about?"

"You already know. It's time."

"Look, I don't know you." T.K. stared at the clock. Twelve-twelve p.m. The clock was rusted on the sides. A fisherman was the clock's face. Two fishing poles were the minute and second hands. "Just let me go. The money is all yours," T.K. shouted.

"I don't want the money, Mr. Kar."

T.K. blinked hard. No one had called him by his last name since...

"That's it, isn't it, Mr. Kar? Thelonious Kar." The voice was kicked up in intensity.

"Did they send you?" T.K. angled around until he was within steps of the door. Now, if someone would just happen by. Maybe. Just maybe.

"Where is the computer, Mr. Kar?"

"Computer?"

"C'mon now, don't shitsham me. I need the damn computer." The voice thundered in the close quarters.

"I don't know what you're talking about."

"I searched your boat. It's not there."

T.K. stared for only a second at his forty-foot dream boat and thought about a scary stranger on board, going through his things.

"Is it all starting to sink in, Mr. Kar?"

"I did what I had to do. And it's done. Now, just leave it at that."

"Oh, no, Mr. Kar. We can't do that. You see, you set the rules. And then, you yourself...well, you know what you did."

"Please, don't harm anyone else. Just promise me that."

"There are no promises kept here, except the one I made with the people you left behind. Now, I'm giving you five seconds, and you tell me where you put the computer and the people you speak about, they will be okay."

There was a long pause, long past five seconds. "I can't do that."

More seconds passed. T.K. looked down at his right palm. Three fishing hooks were pinched tight between his fingers. Hooks facing out. If he could get close enough, a hook in the face would do.

"Okay. I'll tell you where I hid the computer."

For the first time, T.K. heard movement. He turned around. He saw the gun first. The silencer held his attention.

"Okay, where is it?"

T.K. took a chance and started walking toward the man with the gun.

"You can stop right there."

"I have to write it down, give it to you." T.K. slowed his pace but kept walking toward the figure.

"I said stop!"

T.K. stopped his forward progress. He kept his right hand behind him.

"One last time. Where is the computer?"

"Why should I give it to you?"

"Just do as I say."

The bullet hit T.K.'s left shoulder. He dropped like a crate falling off a truck. His first impulse was to reach for his wounded shoulder. In doing so, without thinking, a hook dug into his flesh. With all his strength, T.K. pulled on the hook, ripping his skin, yet still giving him a weapon if he could get close.

"I'm sorry. That was supposed to be a warning shot."

The figure was moving. T.K. looked up. The man was now towering over him, the silencer aimed directly at him.

"Screw you and the computer," T.K. snarled.

"That's such a shame."

The figure used his left hand, grabbing T.K. and rolling him over so he was face-down in his own blood. "Last time, where is the computer?"

"I did what I had to do and I would testify again, you piece of shi..."

Two silent shots and T.K.'s body went limp. The figure looked around for any signs of a witness. Nothing like last time. He heard some footsteps. Had to move. The ice pick came out from his back belt. The figure knelt down and angled T.K.'s chin and neck into just the right position.

19

"What?" Mark David avoided going into hysterics on the phone. "Where did you find them?" He drew a crowd of detectives around him. Dustin, and three others were moving toward his desk, anticipating new information. "Will they let us on the crime scene?" He paused. "Thanks, we will be up there as soon as possible."

David did not hesitate to answer the wondering looks he was facing. "He hit again. Two shots to the head, ice pick, everything."

"Where?" Dustin was closing up his desk drawer, getting ready to move.

"Twenty miles from here. The funny thing is the hit happened almost the same time as Kinnie said she heard him in her house."

Dustin said, "Okay. Two places at the same time. And miles apart. Is she sure it was him?"

"Oh, she's positive. I saw her eyes. Just as scared as the day we first saw her. It was him all right." David headed for the door. "I just don't know how he pulled that off, unless he had an accomplice."

The marina was up the Florida coast, just south of Jupiter. Almost two hours had passed before Dustin pulled into the lot. A trio of detectives was busy in the marina office. Yellow crime tape blocked passage to the area for a solid block. David waited on the outside of the tape for an invitation from the detectives. One of the three approached, holding a large note pad with a black cover. "Welcome to paradise. I'm Connie Johnson." She did not offer her hand, now covered in plastic gloves. Instead, she raised the tape so they could enter. "I'll be the one briefing you. As you can understand, then, I have to get back to my case."

"Did you find a computer?" David asked.

"We're still looking. I read up on your cases. That's part of the pattern but we don't know just yet."

"And the ice pick?"

"Yes, all that is here. We might have some questions for you, if you don't mind." She stopped at the door of the office, making sure they did not step on any evidence. "In here."

Inside, they were directed to the body of T.K. and the marina operator. They were instructed to stay in one spot, while observing the crime techs go over the scene. The bodies were still there, even though they were discovered hours earlier. Detectives always wanted to be thorough.

David saw the ice pick protruding from the underjaw of T.K. There was dirt on his shirt. By a simple comparison, David theorized T.K. crawled along the floor. The same floor dirt was all down his shirt and pants.

"Your time-line," David started. "It's the same as a situation we had in Stilton Bay. Our witness swears he was there at the time."

"The time is the time. We're certain." She pointed to the ceiling. "We're not getting much help here. The cameras haven't been working in this place for years. And the one camera at the end of the marina gave us nothing. No movement."

David sized up her body-language to mean she was done with them for now. "We'll look around. Thanks for your help." They left the immediate scene.

The boat was long. David walked along the dock, trying as best he could to look into the windows, hoping to get a glance at the lower deck.

Dustin posed a question. "Why take the computers?"

David shaded his eyes from the sun. "There's something on them.

Something the shooter doesn't want anyone to see. The computer was taken in each case."

They walked from the bow to the stern looking for a way to look into the boat, knowing they did not have the jurisdiction to step on board. Besides, it was a crime scene. David joined him looking down into the water. "Take some pictures at least. Take lots of pictures."

20

Shannon Tower watched clothes going into a small duffle. "Why don't you pack a suitcase like everyone else?"

Frank Tower ignored the question at first. The last of several T-shirts were stuffed into a side pocket. "Hate'm."

"How long will you be gone this time?"

She had a pout with a certain lure in her eyes, stopping all movement from Tower and almost causing him to toss the bag and move toward an embrace. He closed up the duffle. Another question.

Shannon asked, "Have you given any thought about moving?"

Tower was immersed in the packing. Seconds ticked off and his mind processed the conversations over the last few days. All he could offer Shannon was a blank stare.

She tried again. "The move. I told you I want to move. Sooner rather than later."

"Why leave? You've got your job at the bank, I have my business. Jackie is here."

When he looked into her face, he saw something else. A strong determination to leave.

"This is important to me Frank. I've got some places all picked out. We can fly out..."

"Fly? How far are we talking about?"

"The west coast."

"California?"

"Maybe."

"Maybe?" Tower moved the duffle to the front door. Shannon followed him, matching his steps, then finally taking hold of his hand.

She kissed his fingers. "For me, Frank. I really want this. And we need to do this together. This is a two-person decision."

Tower leaned down and moved into her lips. He pulled back and looked at the face of a person who appeared ready to beg. She pulled him back into her, into the grasp of her arms. The kisses started with soft touches, then proceeded to long embraces. His original intentions were now a muddled mess, as Shannon's movements were convincing him to stay. She let her hands drift down to his belt, opening the buckle, and reaching into pants. He stopped her hands.

"You're making this very difficult," he whispered. "But I have to go."

"No, you don't. You can stay as long as you want, you're the boss of your company. You know you want to stay."

Tower's pulled her hands upward and let them rest on his hips. "I can take my business anywhere, but my license is here. I'd have to start over."

"Then, maybe Tampa, or Naples. I just want to leave here."

"I'll think about it. I promise."

She gave him a half-smile.

Tower buckled the belt. "I don't know how long I will be gone. And since this is a bit sensitive, I won't be calling that much."

"I understand."

"I promise when I'm done, we'll talk about it."

Shannon took her gaze away from Tower. "I like that."

21

"You sure you want to do this, 'cause I can't force you to do anything." Jackie closed the window blind, making the room even darker and shutting out the light. Kinnie Mason was still pondering the question.

"I keep changing my mind. I want to, then I want..."

"I know what you want." Jackie stared through an opening in the blind. "Frank will be here and when he comes, I'll tell you what you need to know."

"You don't understand." Mason looked down at her stash pocket, now empty.

"Forget it, honey. I went through all your stuff. You ain't got no more pills. You want some, you got to go through me and Frank. The pills are over."

"You still don't understand."

"I know all about it." Jackie tried to maintain an even calm in her voice. "If you don't get some pills, your body won't function. I know. I've been there. If you're committed to shaking this, I'm committed to make that happen."

"I feel sick." Mason felt for the couch and put her head down. Four seconds later, she was up and standing. Then she sat back down again.

"He's here." Jackie pulled her gaze from the window and went to the front door. Tower moved in, still looking back over his shoulder.

"The car is in the back," he said. "That way, the place looks like no one is here. We have to keep it that way." He tossed the duffle into a corner. The Glock was tucked into a holster in the back of his jeans. No smiles. Tower had the look of a linebacker about to charge a quarterback. All game-face.

"No phones?" His words were directed at Jackie.

"Just like you said. No phones. I'll give you her cell phone just as soon as I check for some names. We have plenty of food, there's no land-line, no computer. There is a television, but it's not hooked up to cable. I have some portable lights for tonight and we haven't been outside."

"Good." Tower pushed a chair near the front window. He parted the blinds with a coffee mug, allowing him a clear view of the street. Mason approached him.

"Thanks for taking me on as a client."

"No thanks needed. We'll get through this."

"And thanks for the donation to my rehab center." Jackie spread out a sheet over the couch. "Now sit down here. We need to talk."

She sat facing Jackie, looking a bit unsure. "I really need some help Jackie. I need some pills."

"No pills. Listen, honey. This is going to be horrible. Maybe worse than horrible. Withdrawal is a full-body nightmare, like being rolled through a press. So, here's what I got." Jackie pointed to another couch. "I got three sets of clothes for you. In a bit, you're gonna start sweating. You're gonna sweat right through the clothes you got on. When that happens, we'll be ready."

Mason looked at the bowl of bananas like it was filled with mouse droppings. "I'm not hungry. If I do, I'll puke."

"Well, we're ready for that too."

Jackie kept the place dark. She devised a plan with Frank in case Kinnie just decided to up and bolt. They would call Mark David and warn him. For now, they hoped that wouldn't happen and tried to build the small amount of trust between them.

Two hours passed and Mason pulled on the cover for the third time and kicked the blanket off for the fourth. Cold chills had moved into her body, taking up positions in her neck, forehead, back, legs, both arms and stomach. She felt like the flu was wracking her body, causing temperature fluctuations, sending needles of pain into every nerve, blurring her thoughts and cracking her skull with a massive headache. Mason thought it was ten times worse than the flu, like near-death.

She sat up on the couch and whispered. "Every part of my body is yelling, screaming for pills. I need some pills or I won't make it through the day!"

"Sorry, honey. No pills. We got to make it together. We're gonna kick pills ass."

"Right now, they're kicking me."

Jackie helped her into the bathroom. "You're going to take a warm bath. It will soothe some sore muscles. And after that, you've got to drink some more water. Lots of water. Is that clear?"

She didn't seem to hear anything. Her ears ached, each step ached. As she approached the toilet, the one impulse was to throw up. The tub was already filled with water. When did she do that?

Jackie helped her put one foot into the clear water. Kinnie Mason was weak. If the killer smashed into the house now, all would just about be lost. A second foot and both legs now entered the water. Jackie used an old trick. She had a tennis ball handy. When Mason was in place, she took the ball and rubbed her back. The rolling, fuzzy ball was an immediate relief. The look on Mason's face was sheer ecstasy. Jackie hummed a soft tune in her ear and continued to roll the tennis ball, making large round strokes, starting at the neck, then moving to the lower back.

"If I could get just one pill Jackie please, this pain would go away." Mason leaned her head against the tile, her arms soaking in the warmth, taking away the chills. "I'll pay anything. Just get me some pills."

"If you were at my center, we would have a group talk." Jackie rested the tennis ball on a towel. "We can't do that here, so, we're gonna do it the 'Jackie' way. Just us. We'll talk once you dry off."

There was a knock at the door. Jackie jumped. Mason was oblivious to the sudden noise.

"There's something out back. I'm going to check it out." Tower's voice was a whisper.

"Okay." Jackie reached for the towel.

Frank Tower pulled the Glock from the holster and stepped off toward the back door. There was a sound like someone or something making their way through the wooded area behind the house. Tower scanned the tree line.

Nothing.

He waited a full two more minutes before going outside. He held the gun up, police-grip style, and studied the open space like thousands of times when he was on the force. His eyes darted left to right, marking possible hiding places to be checked later and discounting other sections where there was no movement.

There. He heard the noise again. Tower could not see a human form connected with the sound. He moved from protective spot to another, always getting closer to the source of the sound.

Now he was thirty feet away.

Tower leaned over a rock the size of a basketball and found a smattering of leaves and small footprints. He looked up to see a dog running off into the trees. When he returned to the house, Jackie was waiting for him.

"She's having trouble sleeping."

Tower put his Glock back into his jeans. "How long will she go through this?"

A sarcastic grin spread across her face. "The rest of her life. In the short-term, she has three days of this. All rough. The worst mess you can think of, and then she has to be very careful. I went through her phone. Together, we deleted all her drug contacts, and her get-high friends." Jackie looked back at the sleeping singer. "Just one pill, just one and she's in the dumpster again."

"She gonna be okay?" Tower stared down at Kinnie.

"She has a tough road." Jackie looked at the corner of the room. "Thanks for bringing the stuff I asked for."

"No problem."

In the corner were personal items belonging to Mason. Off to one side of the pile was a photograph of Barry Ruddup.

They both watched her. In a rush, like a geyser rising up out of the rocks, Mason rose up suddenly, sitting, eyes open, rigid as slate rock. She turned to them. "I just remembered something important."

22

Detective Mark David studied the photographs from the boat marina as if a clue would jump off the picture. "Anything else from Connie Johnson?"

Dustin walked toward him carrying a file folder. "Her office just called. They are emailing and faxing the bullet results. They are moving really fast." Dustin opened the folder and kept talking. "I added this to the file, but they say the bullets matched the ones in our case. Everything matches. And, like here, there is no computer."

"Is there a way we can find out what chat rooms they were in? Maybe there's some kind of link."

"On it."

"The techs have anything on DNA, surveillance video, anything?

Dustin looked down at the floor before answering. "They got nothing. No DNA cross-contact with the victims. We went as far back as three miles from each scene. Zip. Nothing looks like our guy. Phone records, the same. Nothing seems to link our victims with anyone special. It's like he came out of nowhere."

David remained a calm mixture of contemplating all the facts and trying to move in the right directions. "And I just got word from the feds. They won't be involved anymore. Too much on their plate. We're on our own."

Mark David looked at the crime photos on his desk. "Any more? The FBI was never involved. We're falling behind on this investigation. This guy probably has an idea where to find the next person and we don't."

"What about the people convicted?" Dustin rested his right hand on his weapon. "Shake some trees. See if someone talks."

"We could, but my guess is these marks and contracts were made a long time ago. This guy is operating without any contact with people in the past. They have no idea what he is doing and that's how it's set up."

David stacked the pictures into one small pile. "Cue up the video again from where the stolen car was found. I want to go over it."

23

Kinnie Mason was curled up under a blanket, in the front seat of Tower's car. She twisted in the seat, adjusting and re-adjusting. "I can't get comfortable," she said. Her hair was not combed, she wore no make-up and she continued to rest her head on a dried vomit stain. The smell wafted throughout the car. Tower lowered the window.

"Sorry," she said. "Toothpaste made me sick. Food made me sick. I'm just sick of just about everything. I feel awful. I yawn all the time, but I can't sleep." Her right eye looked darkened. "Every muscle is aching. My joints feel like they're coming apart, and my eyes are always full of tears."

Tower said, "You don't have to do this. We can go back."

"No." The one word was the strongest pronouncement she made all morning. "I have to be here. The police need my help."

Tower looked out at the home of Mason Kinnie. Red evidence tape stretched across the front door. "You tell me when you're ready. I'm in no hurry." Tower walked and checked six bags resting near the door. "Probably fan mail," Mason said.

She was right. Tower checked each bag. They were filled to the top with letters, post cards and even stuffed animals.

"People heard about the shooting, and all the newspaper talk that I was sick. My fans. I love them." She attempted a smile, that never reached more than a quick grin. "One day, I'll answer back, but not now."

"You have a computer?"

"No. Once I got noticed after my first Grammy record, I got off the Net. Had Barry donate my computer once it got wiped. I'm off the grid and like it that way. Don't have to see all the bad stuff people say about me."

She picked at the bandage on her right foot. Since the withdrawal process started, Mason remained barefooted. A thought moved through Tower like an alarm sounding. "You cut your foot on glass. Did you break anything in the house?"

"No."

"What about days ago. You break anything?"

"Nothing. Have a maid. I don't clean much."

"Get up. Come with me."

Mason used all her strength to sit up. She pushed the blanket over to the console, then snatched it back. A full thirty seconds of indecision about the blanket was followed by Mason opening the door, and then closing it again.

"Let me help you." Tower opened the door, took Mason's hand, and eased her out of the front seat. "We can always..."

"I want to see this through. No going back. My new motto."

Tower took her hand and together they walked slow steps until they reached the side of the house. They stopped at the French doors. "I've got to rest." Mason stretched out full on the grass and closed her eyes. Tower sat down next to her. "Just give me a few minutes," she said.

The few minutes became fifteen. Tower sat in silence. Mason angled her arm under her body and pushed up. "Let's go."

Using her key, Tower opened the door and they both stepped inside. "I didn't want to leave you out there..."

"You don't have to explain."

"And this is where you cut your foot?"

She nodded.

Tower studied the floor, then the doors. He rubbed a section of one glass square in the door. He stepped back and watched the sun come through the various panes. For more than seven minutes, Tower examined the door, and then stared into the face of Kinnie Mason. "You see here?" He pointed to the glass. "That's new. This glass doesn't match the rest. You have any work done on the door recently?"

"No."

Tower turned his attention to the rest of the room. "Someone's been in here. They smashed a glass in the French door, replaced it, and did something in your house. And you say you remembered something?"

"Yes. The sound of his voice. Didn't sound right. And when I was at Barry's house." For just a moment her voice cracked.

Tower said, "It's okay. Take your time."

She yawned. "When he was over Barry, he was covered up with something. He had gloves. But I saw the bottom of his palm. His right palm. There was a small mark, like a little star."

"Right palm? Not the left?"

"Right palm. I saw it for just a second."

"Any other marks?"

"Didn't have time. Had to get out."

Mason walked like a puppet on strings. They reached the kitchen. Tower stood next to an island covered in black granite. "So, you heard something right here. Coming from where?"

"That's the thing. I didn't think about it at first. I was so scared. The sound was coming from up above."

Tower focused on the ceiling. He climbed up on the island and stood just inches from a round speaker cover. There were dozens of them spread throughout the house. "You got a screw-driver?"

Mason reached in a junk drawer and tossed him a yellow handled screwdriver. He removed the three screws holding up the plate and took every bit of thirty seconds to remove the round cover.

He looked inside.

Tower took out his phone and waited for someone to come on the line. "Mark. It's Frank. Get your folks out here. I've got a surprise for you."

24

"Thanks for coming forward." Mark David stood among four crime techs, all wearing gloves. They were careful of where they stepped.

"Don't thank me, thank her." Tower pointed to a withered soul in his car, head just barely visible. The stain-laden blanket still smelled putrid, some yards from them.

"She's going through it?" David turned his head from Kinnie Mason.

"Yeah."

"What made you think of the door and the glass?"

Tower started to walk and show him. The crime tape stopped him. "She found the bit of glass on the floor, but nothing was broken. Gave it away. I checked. Bingo."

The detective looked over the group of techs going over the French door. "Good catch."

"You find what I saw in the ceiling?"

Mark David said, "Officially, I can't tell you anything. But just between us, yes, it's a security camera for a front door, placed up there."

"How could it work? She has no wi-fi?"

David pointed to the area where two techs were dusting areas in the ceiling. "This guy put in his own wi-fi hot spot. Then he had the picture routed somewhere, so he could monitor who was walking through the kitchen. So, when she walked to that one spot, he could talk to her through the speaker, just like he was standing next to her. And he could be anywhere."

"Interesting. Works like any security door camera. You go near it, the camera turns on and he has the ability to speak to her directly." Tower pushed to see what he could find out. "So, this explains how he could be in two places at the same time."

"You heard about that?" David looked cautious.

"It's not my case, so if I say too much, it's my ass."

"But that's how it could be done."

David said, "Yes. He could be up there killing his next mark Bonson and speaking to Kinnie Mason here."

"I know your guys will check for prints on that thing, but I'm guessing they won't find any."

Mark David wiped a line of perspiration from his neck. "I can try to trace it, but it was probably stolen from some house."

Tower let his gaze drift over the collection of police cars and crime vans. "And he could be watching us right now?"

Mark David nodded. "He probably was, until we ripped that camera out. But yeah, he could be out there right now, checking us out. Be careful when you leave here."

"I have a plan in place. I don't want to be followed." Tower checked on Mason. She was sleeping. For once, she looked rested. He turned back to David. "You find the victim's computer at the crime scene?"

"I don't think they did. You took note of that?"

"I'm only familiar with Ruddup's case, but I'm guessing he's taking the computers from all of the victims."

"I don't want to answer that directly, but let's just say you're right, what do you think?"

Tower said, "There's obviously a connection to all of the vic's through the computer. Just what, I'm not sure yet. Have you checked earlier email activity from friends and work?"

"Again, I can't answer."

"What about offices?" Tower kept swiveling his head from David to Mason.

"We checked. Seems what we're looking for was on their personal computers and phones."

"I'm assuming you're checking records on what the victims bought in the last few months?"

"For sure."

"You get anything from the scene near Jupiter?"

David checked around as if to see if anyone was watching him, then used his phone to bring up a list. "We just got that."

Tower studied the phone.

"I hope you're sharing fuckin' recipes and not case file." Detective Dustin was less than ten feet from them.

Tower handed back the phone. "Just making sure he has my phone number."

Dustin glared at Tower. "Yeah right, and your ass just grew another hole. Don't sham me, fellas. I know you're sharin' stuff. And I don't like it. Not with this got-away crook."

Tower started to move in on him until David stopped him. Dustin kept going until he was in Tower's face. "We know Tower got away with seventy-thou from the evidence room. We just couldn't prove it."

Tower answered back. "Lie detector says I wasn't involved."

"You're a pro. You know how to scam the detector."

Tower did not back down. "I'll strap up again anytime you want. I had nothing to do with any theft."

"Then why did you leave the force so suddenly?" Dustin bellowed. Two crime techs turned around, and went back to their work.

"Enough." David grabbed the shoulders of both men. "We got things to do here. This isn't the time."

Tower walked away.

Dustin turned to Mark David. "How can you share anything with that idiot?"

David locked stares with Dustin. "He was the best street mind I ever worked with out here. Yes, he was my partner, but I still like to run things by him. Look, he was the one who made the connection on the numbers on the ice picks. The coroner made sure Tower was there, remember? He didn't ask for you; he asked for Tower. If you'd only listen, you could learn things from him."

"Okay, listen to this. I'm your partner now. And I don't share anything else with this guy. Nothing. I didn't trust him when he was on the force and definitely not now."

"Why, because he came from dirt? Crack mom, bad upbringing, all that? He knows how to work a case. Someone set him up on that money deal; I know it."

"The only thing I'm gonna learn from him is how he's gonna get that giant stick out of his ass."

25

Tower drove his blue Honda to a parking garage on Sundrop Road. There, he sat in the car with Mason. He waited for almost fifteen minutes looking for another car, a person on foot, or anyone suspicious. Finding nothing, he walked to another car, pulled out the keys, and opened the door. He moved Kinnie Mason without waking her up, carrying her like a child. In her sleep, she had snaked her arms around Tower's neck and held on. Any sleep for her was rare. The rehab process usually kept her awake. He placed her into the car, and spent the next few minutes again checking for any sign of movement.

Nothing.

He left the Honda and drove out of the garage in a dark-tinted Audi. The car was already packed with a bag of weapons. The Audi was his stash car, always ready for the next assignment. Mason never said a word during the trip back to the safe-house. Tower circled the place three times and double-backed twice before parking the car behind the house.

He kept thinking about the list he saw on David's phone.

"Again, normally, we would do this in a group form, but we don't have that right now." Jackie sat with Mason in the middle of the room. Tower was sitting near a front window, watching.

"In a group counseling session, we could talk with others and share about your addiction. And that's what it is, an addiction. So, what I want you to do is share with me." There was a long pause. Mason ran her fingers over her face. "My name is Kinnie Mason, and I have an addiction to pills and alcohol." There was another long pause. "Well, it all started on a dare. I didn't do pills. I know others had some kind of accident and had them prescribed. Me, someone said I couldn't do just one. I never had a pill before. I tried it. I actually won the bet. I did just one pill. And I loved my vodka. Always have."

Mason started to get up and walk around the room, then sat back down. She yawned twice. Hard. "The problem came the next day. I knew I lost. I wanted two more pills. I liked the way I felt. Confident. I could conquer any big audience. I used them before I went on stage. Became a regular thing. I had the money. I bought as many as I needed. Then Barry found out."

Mason was clear-eyed for the first time since Jackie first met her. Her skin had color. Tower moved as quietly as he could, shifting from the front of the house to the back, from window to window.

"How important did the pills become?"

Kinnie Mason took in a chest full of air. "Everything. My whole life. More important than anything. I had to have my pills. I'd get set with my pills, take off my clothes, get naked, and didn't even want sex. I cut back on them one day and I got sick. Full body sick. It was awful. I decided, I just wanted my pills and vodka. Pills and vodka."

She repeated the words over and over with the same desired care as air and water. Pills and vodka. Pills and vodka. "Barry backed me up. Called the studios when I failed to show up for sessions. Said I was sick when I was passed out. Missed reporter interviews, missed everything. And I missed concerts."

"Like the night I met you?"

"Yes, like that night."

"I want you to take that same desire you had for pills, that same strong feeling, and I want you to replace it, concentrate on something you're fighting for now."

"Fighting for?"

"Yes. Replace that past, replace those past urges and what was important for you in a bottle. What is so important in your life right now that can replace your past? To replace that pill bottle?"

"I dunno. My music?"

"Okay, that's a start. What else?"

"I'm not sure. My music is everything."

"Worth fighting for?"

"Yes."

"Well, fight for it now. Put all your energy behind it. Get behind a great moment in your music life and bring it to the present."

"I can see that."

"Remember the connection you had with the audience. Draw on that. Anything else?"

"I'm not sure."

Jackie raised her voice a bit. "C'mon Kinnie. Fight for something! Beside your music, what is it?"

"I just want to rest but I can't sleep. I'm just fighting to stay alive."

Jackie smiled at her, moved from her chair, and smoothed back Kinnie's dark hair.

26

Tower stepped outside the back door and pulled out his cell phone. He dialed Shannon's number and waited. The call went to voicemail and he realized he was calling during work hours. She would be at the bank and not reachable.

"With any luck, we can turn the corner." Jackie still had a smile on her face.

Tower asked, "She's doing better?"

"Well, the sweats won't go away just yet, but yes, she is doing better. I just have to refocus her mind on things and people and not on the pills and vodka."

"And that takes more than a few days."

"It can take years." Jackie looked at the yard and Tower's car parked under a tree. "Are we safe here?"

"I was thinking about moving us. Staying in one place too long can be a problem."

Worry moved into Jackie's face. "How's Shannon?"

"Just tried to reach her. She's at work. Will try again later."

They both entered the house together. Kinnie Mason was sitting up. "I thought you both just left me here."

Jackie went to the restroom. Tower sat down in the chair next to her. "We're right here."

Mason looked off in the direction of the pile of items Tower was asked to bring. "Can you get me that?" She pointed toward the pile.

"Get you what?" Tower was up and moving.

"My guitar."

He handed the acoustic guitar to Mason. She ran her fingers down the frets and the neck. Her hands moved over the wooden instrument like something she'd done a million times before.

"Haven't picked up this thing in almost a year. I can't believe that." Her fingers strummed a few chords and stopped. She rubbed her fingers into the joints of her arms and shoulders, still dealing with the pain. "In my dreams," she started. "I've had some words to a song bouncing around in my head. Had a few nightmares and lost the words, then I gotm' back."

She strummed a set of chords, the makings of a song and started to hum. No words yet. "It hurts to even smile, but I'm gonna try this."

Tower was mesmerized. She moved her hands with purpose and feeling. Combined with the soft voice, her music transfixed Tower.

Then she sang. "I'm sitting on the edge of your heart." The tone was slow with a touch of the blues. "Watching your love go by. Wondering if you will ever let me back into your life. Back into your life. Back into your life. I'm walking backward, back to your heart. I'm walking backward. Back to your heart."

She played the middle chords, and repeated all the lyrics again. When she was finished, tears streamed down her face.

"That was great," Tower said.

"I heard it all." Jackie emerged from the bathroom.

"I found something I want to fight for."

27

"Take a break. You keep looking out that window." Kinnie Mason wore a white cotton blouse and black jeans. She kept a blanket on her legs. The guitar was resting against the couch. Now, always near her side. She stared at Tower. "We've been here four days now and you never sleep. Just like me."

"Can't take anything for granted with this guy." Tower spoke over his shoulder. His eyes were locked on cars moving down the street.

"What are you doing?" Mason moved closer to him.

"Looking for patterns. I know just about every car that belongs on this block, where they park, when they leave, who should be here."

"And who should not." Her voice had the air of sarcasm.

"Yes. Who should not." Tower turned to her. "Jackie will be back soon. You need anything?"

"Naw. Just you." Mason moved into his space. She got as close as she could get without making him uncomfortable. "You probably saved my life."

"He's still out there."

"Where do you come from, Frank Tower?" She waited a full fifteen seconds. He did not answer.

Mason said, "Okay, I'll go first. My father was black, my mother is white and from Georgia. Her parents came from Spain and Ireland. We traced my dad's line to the Blackfoot Indians. I am a melting pot, Mr. Tower. Mutt family all the way."

Tower was still silent. Kinnie moved in. She angled her lips to meet Tower. He moved back. "I can't do that."

"Do what?"

"You know what I'm talking about."

"It's just us." She tried one more time, pulling Tower closer with her hands. He stood up. "Stop."

"I read about you."

"Read?"

"Jackie let me use her phone. I told her I was just checking for emails from my music company. But I was checking on you. Saw an article about you being named as a suspect in the murder of your mistress."

"I found the killer."

"Sorry about your loss. Did you love her?"

"Almost cost me my marriage. I'm trying to get it back."

Mason looked down at her guitar and turned her gaze to Tower. "Maybe what you need is someone who can sing how she feels. Someone who can really show you how to love."

Tower backed up all the way to the front door. "That was a mistake. There will be no more mistakes in my life."

She was standing with her back to the sun. A hint of the sun shone through the still-closed window blinds. She was backlit. Her hair and face were darkened and in silhouette. Hips, slender legs, all in shadow, except her eyes.

Green.

Her eyes were the only things to pierce the dank quality of the room. Beautiful green eyes staring at Tower. She moved, and the sun showed through her top. Tower could see through the clothing, enough to study the outline of her naked body underneath.

She again stepped toward him. "What you don't understand is when I go after something, you really can't resist, because, Frank Tower, I'm coming after you."

"Think about the problem at hand. You have an addiction. You should be proud of what you're doing so far. I'm helping you, but don't let that translate into something else."

A noise made Kinnie freeze.

Jackie came through the back door. "I wasn't followed. I promise. Parked in the back, next to you." Jackie stared at them both. "Something I'm missing?"

"No." Tower moved back to his position near a front window. His study of cars moving down the street, continued. Then, he stood up abruptly. "I'll be in the back yard. Be right back."

He pulled on his cell phone as he closed the back door. He tapped the numbers and waited. The voice on the phone was pleasant. "South-North Regional Community Bank."

"Yeah, this is Frank Tower. I'm looking for my wife, Shannon."

"Hello, Mr. Tower. She's been out sick. Due back, I think tomorrow." Tower thanked her and tapped Shannon's cell number.

"Frank?"

"Shannon, what's up? They tell me you're sick."

"I'm not sick, Frank."

"What's going on?"

"I haven't called them yet but I'm quitting my job."

"Quit? Why?"

"On second thought, I'm just going to leave."

"Shannon. What is going on?"

"It's all my fault, Frank. All my fault."

"What are you talking about?".

"What I told you about me. My life. Everything. It's all a lie." There were no sounds of tears coming through the phone speaker. Shannon's voice had the calm dryness of a person in control. "When I get off the phone, you won't be able to find me. I'm wiping away my past here. Just forget about me."

"Shannon! Wait. Stop for a second. Meet me somewhere. Let's talk about this. If you're worried about some past, I don't care. I love you."

"You sound sincere, Frank. We were close to getting back to just us." There was a long pause. "I have to go."

"Why?"

"I don't have a choice. He's close and I have to go."

"Who, Shannon?" Tower's voice thundered in the open yard. He could hear Jackie coming through the back door. Her face was covered in worry lines.

"I thought I would be safe, being married to a police officer. Even now, I thought they would never find me. But now...I don't know. Just one thing. You are free, Frank Tower. I am releasing you and you don't have to worry about me anymore."

"Let me help you. I am not going to abandon you. Are you at home? I'll be right there."

Shannon's voice was almost a whisper. "The man with the ice pick. You see, I'm next on his list. He's down to one last mark. Me. I'm his target and if I don't leave now, he will kill me."

Dial tone.

28

Tower gave instructions to Jackie, telling her to return to her rehab center. Kinnie Mason stood in the middle of the room confused. She watched him throw a few things into the duffle he brought with him.

"What are we doing?"

"Like I said, gather up what you can. We have to leave. Now."

"But what's going on? You never explained."

Tower said, "My wife is in danger. I have to help her."

"But I'm in danger. It's from the same guy?"

"Yes." Tower slung the duffle over his shoulder.

Worry creeped into Mason's face. "So. rather than hide from this guy, you're going to maybe bring me even closer to him by running after your wife?"

"I don't want to leave you here by yourself. The police can't put an armed protection around you like I can. And you are much better off by my side, then on your own."

Mason let the reasoning sink in. She was still sore from withdrawal. The warm baths seemed to be working. She told Jackie her desire was less, yet if she got close to a pill, the lure might be too strong to pass up. She gathered up the blanket, now washed three times to remove any smell.

Everything was packed into a large purse. When she reached the door, Mason stopped.

"There is one thing I have to take with me." She ran to the couch and grabbed her guitar. "Not going anyplace without it."

29

Frank Tower circled his home three times before parking four-hundred-feet from the front door. He sat in his car, watching.

"What are we waiting for?" Kinnie Mason moved around in her seat, shifting, yet she never seemed comfortable.

"Doing surveillance on my own home. Making sure we were not followed." He opened the glove box, reached in and pulled out a .38, complete with an ankle strap. Kinnie watched, as he tied on the small weapon, snug just about his right shoe. The Glock was still tucked into the back of his pants. "Let's go."

Tower was a few feet from his door when he turned to Mason. "Stay close to me."

"I'd love to."

Tower was about to use his key, then noticed the front door opened with just a touch. The Glock came out of the holster and he held up the weapon in front him, police-grip style, leading the way. Kinnie stayed right on his back, eyes moving left to right. He went from room to room, then finally put the weapon back into the holster.

"There's no one here."

She followed him into the family room. Tower went to a granite island.

He snatched up the travel brochures Shannon showed him days earlier. California, Seattle, Scottsdale.

"Is that where she went?" Mason studied the pamphlets.

"That," Tower took a long sigh, "was left there to throw off anyone who came in here. She's not headed to any of those places."

"You sure?"

"Positive. The question is, where did she go?" Tower went into the bedroom. "The computer is gone."

"Just like Barry."

"Just like all the cases."

He searched the room, going through the closet, taking an assessment on what was left, what was taken. "Her warm weather clothes are still here. So, she didn't head to a cold area. And I don't think she is going to the west coast of the United States."

Tower took his time going over the chest-of-drawers.

"What are you looking for?"

"We had an agreement, a way to leave secret messages for each other. Worked out great last year. I was able to warn her about something."

"Anything?"

"No."

"I want you to look for any cosmetics. Smell around, check for any perfume. Anything that might help us."

"And you?"

"Just checking around. If you see anything, yell."

Tower went to the garage. Everything looked to be in its proper place. The search took several minutes. He went back into the house and heard a noise, like something being dropped on the tile.

"Dammit." Tower ran to the bathroom. He found Mason on the floor, hands reaching out, trying to pick up one of three tablets rolling around on the tile squares. The amber-colored pill container was on the sink. The cap was also on the floor. The pills, marked for a pain medication, had been opened.

He shouted. "Get up! Get up now!"

Tower grabbed her shoulder, lifting her up and away from the pills. She twisted out of the grip and landed hard on the floor, mouth open, tongue out, licking the floor, like an ant-eater, trying as best she could, to sweep up one of the pills. She kept kicking her legs, trying to get some distance from Tower. Her right hand moved in a quick motion to direct at least one of the pills into her open mouth. Mason got closer. Her tongue kept darting forward snake-like, moving across the floor, leaving a trail of saliva on the dark and white squares. Tower grabbed her again, this time wrapping his arms around her chest. She started swinging. Arms, hands, like a windmill in over-drive. "I want the fucking pills. Just one!"

"No more pills!" Tower picked her up off her feet and started moving backward, away from the bathrooms. Her face was a snarling, wild-eyed, collection of swinging arms and yells.

"Fix me! Fix me now! Just one pill. Just one." She started beating his chest with her fists, landing fists on Tower's face and arms.

He did not stop until he was all the way back in the living room, where he plopped her onto a wrap-around couch. He got up close, until he was in her face.

"There is a guy out there, just waiting to kill you. And now he is after my wife. The thing that is stopping me from finding him is you. I can't find her and help you unless you stop trying to poison yourself."

Her hair was all over. She sat there, breathing heavy. The long strands covered her face. The words came out through a batch of dark hair. She looked like some beaten monster, finally spitting out bits of dirt from the bathroom floor. "I'm broken Frank. Fix me."

"You're about to die a horrible death unless you get control of yourself. I can't leave you. In an hour, you'll do something to let him know exactly where you are and then he'll have you."

"I'm stuck." She used her hand to remove a piece of hair from her mouth.

Tower kept his voice at an even keel. "This might not sink in right away, but yesterday patrol units found two parents in the front seat of their car. Both dead. Overdose. Their kids were in the back. We've had fourteen cases just like that across the state. Pill overdoses. This stuff is too powerful. And Kinnie, you're next."

She blew part of the strands out of her way and used her hand to swipe away the long locks from her face. Her eyes looked like anger mixed with frustration. Tower had no idea if his words meant anything to her.

"I went through all of this with my mother." Tower's voice had the sound of a person who went through ten ordeals. "I tried to stop my mother. Just like you. Back then, it was crack. She always picked the drug over me. Can't tell you how many times I was left alone."

"I'm sorry."

"You're doing great. Or, was. Four days and no pills."

"Yeah, but one pill. Just one and I'm in the pit." Her breathing returned to some form of normal.

A thought hit Tower. "Get up. Come with me."

He held out his hand. She took it. Together, he led her into the bedroom. "What do you have in mind, Frank?"

"You can stop right there. I can't trust you out of my sight right now. Sit on the bed."

"And what's next?" A sly smile spread across her face.

"Nothing. Sit on the bed."

Tower went through Shannon's side of the chest-of-drawers. He carefully checked the arrangement of bras and personal items. A map was folded tucked inside a pair of shorts. Tower held the map up to the light.

"Let's go. I think I know where she's headed. But I need to talk to someone first."

30

Tower and Mason sat in his car, outside the police department. "C'mon Mark." Tower was pounding on the dashboard.

"Who are we waiting for?"

"This won't take long." He turned to Mason. "Here's the deal. I have to trust you. You already trusted me with your life. But you have to help me. I can't find Shannon and watch you destroy yourself, looking for pills. I've never had to do this before, but maybe we should end this. You go and do whatever you want, and I've got to find my wife."

Tower pointed to the street.

She shook her head. "No, I don't want to leave. I don't want to be alone."

Tower said, "You made the choice. The drugs over me. I can't compete with that. Jackie can't be here to counsel you all the time. You can hit the streets."

"No. I'll stop. I promise. No more drugs."

"How can I believe you?"

"Believe it." She leaned toward him, pressing her head into his chest. She wrapped her arms around him.

"Okay. You can stop. You have this one last chance. I have to watch you and focus on Shannon."

"I won't be a bother. Watch me."

"What's up Frank?"

Tower turned to find Detective Mark David staring at him. Tower said, "I need a moment." He stepped away from the car, leaving Mason, and did not stop until he was out of her ear-range.

"I need your help."

"Sure. What is it?"

"Are you any closer to finding the hit-man?"

"You know I can't say much, but we're making progress."

"He's after Shannon."

"What?" David noticed his voice was loud and toned down his voice. "Why do you say that?"

"She told me. She is his last mark." Tower tried to figure out what bit of information to give him first. "For weeks, she's been trying to convince me to move away. Get out of town. I didn't pay it much attention. Then, she told me her life with me was a lie and that this guy was after her. Now, she's missing."

"She say why?"

"No. And that's why I need your help. How does she figure into all of this? What did she testify to, and who might be after her now."

"I have to bring this to the group."

"No!"

"Why not?"

"I'm trusting you, Mark. Just us. Give me two days to find her. If I don't find her on those two days, do what you want. But I need you to find out about Shannon. What am I missing? What was her life before me?"

"I don't know."

"Please Mark, I'm asking you. Please do this. Just two days. Give me some information so I can protect her from this guy." Tower waited for a response. He paced a few steps while looking at Kinnie in the car.

A look of worry was burned into David's face. "If they find out."

"They won't find out. Just search your computers and tell me what you find out. Then, give me some time. That's all I'm asking."

"Okay. But you gotta keep me in the loop. Everything you're doing. Is that clear?"

"Got it."

"Give me one hour and I'll get back to you. How do I reach you?"

Tower handed him a cell phone. "Great," David said. "I'm using a burner phone."

"You know the routine. When we're done with it, toss it."

"One hour."

Tower shook his hand. "One hour."

"Hey Tower, I see you're still with the drug queen. Still bangn' her, huh?" Dustin was ten feet away and closing in.

"That's enough Dustin." Mark David positioned himself between them. Dustin walked toward Kinnie. "Hey, you know this guy has a reputation? And then you know what happens?"

"That's enough," David was shouting.

Dustin kept going. "His old case? His client gets murdered. So, you better watch your ass."

Tower moved past David, fists balled, ready to swing at Dustin.

"Stop!" David was between them, holding off two line-backer-sized men ready to throw punches. "Settle down. We're right in front of the station. Calm down!"

Dustin moved back first. Tower relaxed his fists. A strong push from David sent Dustin back toward the front door. He turned to Tower. "I got your back. For now. One hour."

31

"Where are we going?" The car window was down. Mason let the wind sort through her hair.

"We are headed to a marina. I have a hunch."

"Based on what?"

"Two things. A pinhole on a map I found in Shannon's stuff. And a copy of a receipt from the marina shop. There's something there and I'm going to find it."

A turquoise Atlantic Ocean was on their right, as they traveled north on A1A. Farther out, the ocean gave way to shades of purple and Navy blue, as the deeper the water, the darker the color of the sea. Frigate birds swooped and dove in attack patterns, hitting the water with a certain force, then pulling up toward the sky, a fish caught in their beaks.

Mason started humming a song. The tune was the same one she played with the guitar. "I'm working on it," she said. She sang lyrics. "I'm sitting on the edge of your heart, watching your love go by. Wandering if you will give me a second try. A second try."

She stopped for a moment. "I'm still working on the words." Her singing began again. Words carried on the brine-filled air. "My tears are falling up. Up. Up. My tears are falling up to you." She finished.

"For Barry?" Tower never took his eyes off the road.

"Yes. Jackie always says you have to fight for something. Even though he's gone, I'm doing everything I can for Barry. And if that means no more pills, then it's no more pills." Her hair kicked up with the breeze and flowed with the gusts. "And I'm fighting for my music. I have to claim it back."

She closed her eyes.

An hour later, Tower pulled into the marina and parked. "Stay in the car. Be right back."

The marina store was open again. A woman with her hair tied in the back, was behind the counter. Her eyes stayed transfixed on Tower as he entered the store.

"Can I help you?" She stayed in one position, Tower reasoned because there was probably a shotgun now under the counter.

"The name is Tower. Frank. I'm here looking for someone. I'm a private investigator."

"Don't know too much. I wasn't here when..." She caught herself. For just a second, her voice went weak, then she straightened up. "Wasn't here when it happened."

"Not here to ask any questions about that. I understand the boat owner, Mr. Kernan Bonson bought some equipment here." Tower tapped on his phone and visually went over a list. "Bought a new boat anchor and a box."

"How do you know that?"

"I'm paid to know things. If I find out something, I share it with police."

"You helping them?"

"In a manner, yes." Tower looked around the store. "I'd like to buy some things. I want that snorkel mask over there and those flippers."

She turned and pulled them down from a rack behind her and rang them up on the register. "Anything else?"

"Yes, but when I get back." He moved his cell phone in her direction. "This is a picture of her."

The woman shook her head.

Tower paid in cash and let her know he didn't need a bag. Once he got back to the car, he was surprised to see Mason was still there. "I need you to watch our stuff while I go swimming."

"Okay."

Tower checked his watch. More than two hours had passed and no call from Mark David. He was parked close to Bonson's boat. Tower changed in the back of the car, getting into swim trunks and piling his valuables under the front seat. The pictures from the detective were his tip. Tower checked the surface, took a deep breath, then turned his back to the boat and slipped into the brackish water. Tower was at ease in the dark green water. A quick check showed the hull needed a cleaning. He grabbed the chain line and followed it down fifteen feet until he hit the sandy bottom. Tower swept the area with his hands, moving sand from where the anchor should be located. He kept removing sand and started to feel the strong need to breathe. He stayed down, determined to keep searching. Tower kept pulling back sand until he hit something solid. The object was not the anchor.

Tower found a case.

He unsnapped the case from a hook and started moving upward. When he reached the surface, Kinnie Mason was waiting with a towel.

"What is that?"

"We need to find out."

Tower felt around the edges of the case. No lock. The case was sealed. When Tower hit the clasps, the case yawned open with a noise. Everything inside was dry.

"How did you know?" Mason stood over the case.

"I just had a hunch. If Bonson knew others were being killed and the laptop was so important, he might not leave it on the boat. And then I thought, where could he hide it?"

He felt around the case, finding a bill-of-sale for the boat, an old ring, a few nautical maps and photographs. Tower stopped searching.

Tower found a laptop.

He hesitated and thought about his next move. Trying to open the laptop could be considered tampering with evidence in a multi-murder case. Worse, he might be charged with impeding an investigation. He was driven by something else. Finding Shannon before anyone else. Tower pulled the laptop out of the case and placed it on the trunk of the car, letting it rest on a piece of plastic.

"I need some help."

Mason finished the last piece of a banana and tossed the peel into the water. "Whatcha need?"

"I have to figure out the password for this guy. Not gonna lie to you, I might be arrested for this. I need you to look the other way."

"I'm in this no matter what."

"Think about what you're saying. Sit in the car, turn on the air. Let me do this alone."

"No." Before Tower spoke another word, Mason was reaching for the computer. "I'll type. You throw some passwords at me."

Tower held up his hands to stop her. "Hold on." He went to the car and pulled out two pairs of plastic gloves, giving a set to Mason. They pulled them on.

Tower took out his phone and went over the notes he got from Mark David. "You can start with his birthday."

"No one does birthdays." Mason typed in the numbers given to her. "Nothing."

"What about his daughter?" Tower flipped down and retrieved the name from the file.

"Naw. That's not it." In the next twenty minutes, Tower tried every name or combination and nothing worked. He checked his watch again. No word from Mark David. Not good. Tower studied the activity of the marina. Boats bobbed silently in their slips.

The boat.

Tower checked the name of the boat. Forever Sunset. He instructed Mason to try the name.

She yelled. "We're in!"

Tower took the laptop from her. He checked the files. Fortunately, there were not that many. One file just had the number one. He opened the file.

"This is a link." Tower clicked on the link. He was taken to a website. He read more. "This has to be it. This is a chat room and note board."

He read down the line and saw a series of conversations. "Looks like he gave himself the name of PP9, whatever that means. But you can see the back-and-forth between PP9 and others."

Kinnie Mason had a glow in her face. "The guy who killed Barry has to be one of these guys."

"Exactly."

Tower stopped. His finger almost shook as he pointed the few lines to Mason. "Shandrip. That's Shannon. She's in here."

"Shandrip?"

"We met on the beach. Dripping wet. She has used this name before. Shannon dripping wet. Or Shandrip." Tower studied the conversations. "We have to match up the victims with the names in this chat room."

They both started reading through conversations. "PP9 is talking with someone named InfoLeader."

Tower placed his finger on the monitor screen. "There are conversations here with InfoLeader talking about hooking these people up with family. That's important."

Mason said, "Everyone has family."

"Not if you're in witness protection. You're cut off from family. All these names were trying to connect back with loved ones, and it looks like Info-Leader was supposed to be the key in finding family members."

"And that included Shannon?"

"Yes. See here? Shandrip talks about a planned meeting on the west coast of Florida. Only there's a problem." Tower reads through more of the conversations. "There is talk of one person being killed. InfoLeader tries to low-ball it, but they are all scared. That's how Shannon knew about the killings. It's all on the note board."

His burner phone rang and the woman from the marina was approaching at the same time.

Tower put the phone to his ear. "Yeah."

"Frank, it's Mark. We need to talk. Now. This is important."

"Can't you tell me over the phone?"

"I cannot. You need to hear this for yourself. In person."

"You want to meet me somewhere?"

"Yes, but we have to make this official. You remember Mo? From Homeland Security? She has to be there."

"What? Why her? What's going on and tell me right now."

"I can't Frank. We need to talk. Some of this is classified. In person."

The woman stood in front of Tower. "Hope I'm not interrupting."

"Yes. No problem. What is it?"

"Sorry to bother, can you show me the picture again?"

Tower took out a photograph of Shannon and let her see the image."

"Yes, that's her. Sorry, I didn't catch it before."

"She was here? You sure?"

"Oh yes. I thought about it and I had to come out and tell you."

Tower spoke into the phone. "Can't talk to you right now. And I thought we were going to keep this between us?"

"Frank, you don't understand. This is vitally important. We need to talk and I can't get into it over the phone."

"I'll talk to you when I can. You're going to get a call from someone. I'm leaving you some evidence."

"Evidence? Where?"

"You will get a call. I found this and I'm giving it to you. Please give me more time."

"We don't have any time. Frank, we go back a long way. You have to trust me. We need to talk. And right now. Where are you. I will come to you."

"You will get a call." Tower put away the phone and turned to the marina clerk. "When did you see her?"

"This morning. She was asking about my friend who was murdered."

"And what did you tell her?"

"She asked about his other place, where he stays when he's here." The woman paced a few steps. "And then later, the man came."

"What man?"

"Well, your Shannon left here an hour ago. A man also came this morning, looking for her. I'm sorry I should have told all this before when I met you, but I wasn't sure."

"What did this man look like?"

"Hard to tell. He had a hat and sunglasses. Cloth around his face. Said he was protecting himself from the sun." She stared at the ocean, as if going over more thoughts in her head. "But what I noticed most was what was on his hand."

"What was that?"

"A small star."

32

"I'm not going to tell you to slow down. I like going fast." Kinnie Mason started to roll the window down.

"Don't do that." Tower's quick glance at the dashboard showed he was doing more than one-hundred miles-per-hour.

"Sorry about that." A Florida landscape flashed by. Glimpses of door fronts and stores moved past so fast, no one had time to read them. They went around two cars and Mason tried, but could not get a fix on the driver or a model. "This is a rush. I like it."

Tower slowed when he approached Federal Highway, also known as A1A. He turned left and kept within the speed limit. "No more racing?" Mason said to the window.

"We're gonna get out in a minute. I'll park the car near the place. You stay with the car." Tower turned to her. His face had the burned stare of someone ready to do anything.

Mason offered a plea. "I won't leave the car. I promise."

Tower turned left, or west, traveled a slow pace down the street and parked under a crepe myrtle tree. He pulled out his gloves and the laptop and started tapping keys.

"Whatcha doing?" Mason hovered over the monitor.

"Making one last check before I get out." Tower used the password he had and logged in. He started checking the screen. "Looking for Shannon," he said.

He kept scrolling down the chat room. Then back up. "Nothing new." He logged off and shut down the computer. "Keep watching the street. Anyone look suspicious..."

"I know. Duck down."

Tower got out of the car and put his hand briefly on his Glock to re-check its location. He was four houses down from the exact address.

Kinnie looked at him like she was studying a crowd before a concert. "Ya gonna wait for police?"

"I don't want to see them. If they find me, they will shut me down. Limit what I can do. I want to stay a step ahead of them or I might lose Shannon. Can't take that chance." Tower walked along the side of the house. The place was a two-story stucco with a large window casement. The house was built for the view of the Atlantic. There were no cars parked out front. Still, he treated the scene like someone was waiting for him. He placed the Glock at his side, his finger just off the trigger. He leaned against a wall and placed his ear on the cold stucco exterior. Tower stood there for almost a minute, listening for any sounds coming from inside. Hearing nothing, he moved to a window. Another minute went by before he glanced inside. The room looked empty. He ducked under the window and moved quickly to the back yard. The space was small. A patio table was covered in dead-brown sea grape leaves. The yard was covered with them.

Tower tried, but any movement among the dry leaves gave off the sounds of his feet. He checked the back glass. There was a floor to ceiling wall of glass. Tower figured they must be connected to a remote control to open the sliders to the beauty of the ocean and take in the breeze.

Again, no one inside. Then he stopped.

There was a shoe on the floor, next to the couch. He was sure the shoe belonged to Shannon. She was here. The shoe was a six-inch heel variety and not one she wore traveling along the coast of Florida. He had a deci-sion to make. Tower could break into the place and possibly break more laws or just back off.

"Don't do it." The voice came from Detective Mark David.

Tower put away his Glock. A former officer gauging a detective. A stand-off. Neither stare gave away anything. "Before you ask me what am I doing here..."

"I know what you're doing here. And she's not here." David pointed to his unmarked way off in the distance. "You underestimate me. I've been here, checked the place and now I was staking it out, hoping someone would show up." David cocked his head, leading Tower to the patio table. "We really need to talk."

"Where is everyone? You already knew about this place, didn't you?" Tower looked around the house and saw no backup.

"The team went to the marina. I went ahead to this location. And, I was hoping to catch up to you." David's face took on a serious look. He ran his fingers over face.

"Is Shannon safe?" Tower couldn't wait any longer.

"We don't know."

"Then, what is she involved in?"

"I'm getting to that."

Tower shouted at him. "Tell me!"

"Did she tell you about this place?"

Tower calmed down. He shook his head, walked to the side of the house and down the block. Kinnie Mason was in the front seat, looking like she was straining her eyes to find him. He waved to her and she nestled back into the seat. When he returned, David was sitting. Even from a distance, Tower could see Mason had an expression of mixed thoughts. She fidgeted in the seat, and looked like her mind was full of demons about to be unleashed. The question was, could she hold on? Right now, she was winning, but for how long?

"I want to compare notes." Tower looked like the kid on the block, almost begging for someone to buy his cookies so he could go to camp.

Mark David told him, "You know I can't do that."

Tower said, "I shared everything with you."

"Everything?"

"Just about." Tower looked at the pristine houses. "You check the neighbors?"

"All of them. No one saw or heard anything."

David asked, "How is she doing?"

"Better. Much better. But she's one pill from falling back into a shitpile."

A new voice, a woman, joined the conversation. "I can fill him in." Tower had seen her once before, on another case.

David pointed to a chair. "Morning Mo."

Molissa Grant sat down. Her hair was pulled back into a tight bun. She wore her usual starched white shirt, this time without the blue business jacket. Grant's steps matched her general outlook; quick and no-nonsense. Her gait was much more than a walk. Tower sensed she was actually marching, or a semblance of marching, probably left over from her six years following her father's lead, in the military.

"Homeland Security knows about Shannon?" Tower was getting agitated.

David waited until she was seated. "Mo knows about the case from the beginning."

Mo wore no lipstick, had short nails and her left knee was scuffed. "First, we're going to get her back. We're all working on this."

"If she can outrun him. He's gone down his list. Shannon is the last one." Tower's eyes scanned his surroundings. A force of habit.

Mo took in a deep breath of oven-fried Florida air. "Shannon was the key witness in what we called, Operation Blue Dumpster. This was a west coast deal where a Ponzi scheme stretched from L.A. to Seattle. It involved dummy companies tied to kickbacks, with a promise to give investors up to twenty-percent return on their money. The whole thing was uncovered by Shannon and she called us." Tower scratched his chin. "I never heard anything about this in the news."

Mo continued. "We kept everything sealed. You see several government agencies retirement funds and two defense contractors got caught up in this. There was a phone call to keep the media out of it, so we did. Shannon arranged it so everything went through her. She was the key."

"And people went to jail?" Tower asked.

"Oh yeah." Mo smiled for a millisecond. "Three people were tried in a secret court. No one heard about it. The whole thing was sealed due to national security. We gave Shannon a new life. She moved here."

"Blue Dumpster?"

Mo's delivery was dry as the sun blasted sand. "Sometimes they shredded key materials. Stuff that would send them to prison. They always put it in a blue dumpster. Only, Shannon made sure to keep the real stuff and cut up meaningless paperwork."

"So, Shannon is not her real name?"

"No." Mo took her time. "Her name is Rene Wilson. She was in witness protection and she was given a new life."

Tower had a lot more questions. "Did she stay in protection?"

"No. She decided to leave witness protection in the summer, four years ago."

"That's the summer we first met. We got married three months later."

Mo looked directly into Tower's stare. "She contacted us and said she was leaving protection after she met you. That you were once a police officer and she felt safe."

Tower stood up. "Great. And how safe is she now? I don't know where she is, and I can't protect her. Some husband."

David grabbed his arm. "Stop beating yourself up. You didn't know."

"But I should have done something. She kept talking about moving. I didn't listen."

David remained quiet, letting Mo do all the talking. "She's good at keeping secrets. Even from you. The only reason we can tell you this now is because she signed a waiver when she left us."

"Waiver?"

"Yep. If you ever found out something on your own, she wanted me to fill you in. And I am doing that now."

Tower started moving toward his car. Again, only Mo spoke. "If you're thinking your old partner let you down, Mark didn't know anything about this." She walked until she got directly in Tower's face, bringing his walk to a stop. "And if you're thinking about going after her, forget it."

"She's my wife."

Mo kicked a tiny lizard away from her feet. "I shared with you. You have anything to share with me?"

Tower felt cornered. "I found a laptop. It was in the sand under Bonson's boat. Locked in a box."

She moved a bit closer to him. "You tamper with evidence?"

"I wore gloves. I tried to protect chain-of-custody."

Her voice ticked up a bit in volume. "You get into the computer files?"

"I'm trying to find my wife."

Now she was shouting. "Did you get into the file?"

"Yes."

Mo said, "We could arrest your right now for obstruction. When you found that computer, you should have turned it over to us. Instead, you messed with it. You know better than that. You broke the chain of evidence."

Tower's personal safety did not matter to him right now. His goal never changed. Find Shannon. He tried to find the words to convince her he was not meaning to jeopardize the case. "I was going to turn it over to you. It's in my trunk. I'll give you the keys. My prints are not on it."

"You're walking a very fine line right now. I would arrest you but this is going to be your last warning." Tower could see her jaw muscles tighten. Mashed and gritted teeth. "If you make another move like this, so help me." She didn't finish.

"I'll keep you informed." Tower lied.

Mark David said, "The woman at the marina told us you were in the water. We knew you were up to something."

Tower replied, "I have to get her back."

Mo shot him a look. "Let us do that."

"You, help her? Like you helped the other victims? Now all deceased?"

Mo's chin took on a rock firmness. "I can't let you look for her. You'll just get in the way."

"Shannon, or Rene, I don't care, I'm going to find her. If you want to arrest me, go ahead. Just know I'm not going to stop till I find her. I know she's out there."

Mo studied Tower. "The keys."

Tower tossed his car fob to Mo. She caught it and didn't flinch. "You find anything on it?" she asked.

Tower remained silent. Mo persisted. "Our people are working on it, but if you have any info, let me know now."

Still nothing from Tower. Mo's voice again raised to the level of anger. "You keeping things from us will not go well. I don't care if your wife is missing."

Tower stood his position. Admitted to nothing.

Mo calmed down. "Did you ever stop to think, maybe there's a reason she doesn't want you to find her?" Mo scratched an imaginary bug on her shoulder. Even through the starched blouse, Tower could see Mo spent time in the gym.

"What is that supposed to mean?"

Mo signaled to Mark David and the two of them started toward Tower's car.

"What is that supposed to mean!" Tower was talking to their backs. The pair split at the sidewalk, moving toward unmarked cars. Tower caught up to Mo. "Was she working on another operation?"

"Did you say was? Or is?" Mo turned away, no longer interested in Tower.

Mark David approached him. "Look, we're waiting on a search warrant to go into the house. They are telling me, years ago, this was her house. We want the warrant to make sure the case is tight. Don't screw with her again."

"Or else?"

"She'll put you in cuffs."

33

The Figure placed a gloved hand on the window and parted the blinds just wide enough to study the car with the woman who couldn't sit still in the front seat. "Dammit, too many people around." A column of light exposed his wrist to the sun and the star tattoo. A primal grunt came from the Figure. He counted three people who went around to the back of the house across the street. He smiled, stood back for a moment to study his surroundings, and prided himself on picking a place with a great view for his surveillance.

The Figure looked like a space man. His feet were covered in hospital-like booties. A similar covering was on his head. He was wearing a body-suit in the same material. And the gloves.

"Just leave her alone for just a few minutes," he whispered to the curtain. He turned and took his attention away from Kinnie Mason some eighty-feet away and concentrated on the homeowner tied up in ropes on the milk-white carpet. The man had the wide-eyed terrified look of a someone who had fallen five floors and was about to hit the pavement. Each of his wrists had rope burns and cuts. The shirt pocket was torn from the initial encounter with the Figure. Once the brief struggle was over, he was placed on his left side. Spittle rolled down the left side of his face because of the gag in his mouth. A pool of drool seeped into the usually iceberg-white rug. His feet were tied behind him and the rope connected to his belt, hog-tied style. The man looked like he was trying to say something. The Figure mocked him.

"Whatya tryin' to say? Let you go?" The Figure angled his body so he would not be seen from the street and dropped down on his knees and leaned in close. The words came out low, like a hissing sound, through gritted teeth. "I waited till after the police checked this house. Smart of me, wasn't it? Then I came in. You know, you should always lock your back door." The figure pulled out a long-bladed knife and placed the weapon on the carpet with the blade facing the man's face, perhaps ten feet away. "No guns or ice pick for you. That's for the others. Just stare at this and don't even think about trying to get up."

The Figure looked at the pictures on the wall. Family photographs. The carpet victim with wife and sons somewhere in the woods and not in Florida. The pictures gave the Figure a whole history of his victim. College graduations photographs, right down to pics of favorite vacations. The rooms had already been checked out. Now empty, each son had a room full of baseball trophies and track ribbons. An urn rested on a table in the hallway.

"Wife dead?" The Figure picked up the urn, adorned with blue flowers on a white background. He pretended to drop the urn, then caught it just before hitting the floor. "Nice catch, huh?" He smiled to reveal green-colored teeth, set in a chin of hard stubble.

The Figure walked back to the window. There was a gathering. Three police-looking people and the eyewitness in the car. All the cars drove away in a slow procession.

"Ah, they're gone." The Figure walked to the knife and held it up. The light glinted off the blade. "Here's how it's gonna work. I'm putting this eye-picker back on the floor. Every so often, I will move it a bit closer to you. Closer and closer, until you smell the old blood on this thing. Until then, I've got to watch this house. I'm waiting for someone."

34

Kinnie Mason moved to let the wind rearrange her hair. The brine-scented air gave the place its own aroma. Tower got behind the wheel and started driving south.

"Where we going?" Mason closed her eyes in the car-driven breezes.

"We're going to get a hotel room." Tower drove from the road to the side streets, looking for a big-box hotel.

Mason tried to smile. "I still can't sleep. My joints are better but I can get really sore at times."

"You're doing great. Just fine."

Within the hour, Tower checked in. The location had five floors. Tower took a room on the second level. Easy access to the street, yet not too close for an intruder. Mason let her body flop on the clean sheets. "You don't want to go back to Stilton Bay?"

"I want to stay in this area. If Shannon is here, then this is where I want to be."

The view from the hotel room gave Tower a way to check cars coming in and leaving. He was in a room on the second floor, next to the stairwell.

"You take either bed. I'll sleep in the bathroom." Tower pointed to the door. "If anyone comes through that door, I want to be the first thing they see."

"The bathroom?" Mason puckered her lips into a pout. She reached out her hands. "Come sleep in the other bed. I won't bite." Her eyes had the gleam of a lie.

"I feel better knowing I can get to anyone coming in the door." Tower opened the bathroom door wide. "I'll put down some blankets. I'll be fine."

Mason started rubbing her shoulder, stopping when Tower looked in her direction. "I still feel sore. I'm not through this yet. All my joints are aching during the night."

"If you promise not to do anything, I'll rub your shoulder and back."

She immediately rolled face down on the bed. Tower took his time, gently moving from her neck, down and across her back shoulder blades and the backs of her arms. Mason let out soft moans. For the first time in a long while, she closed her eyes and actually felt like sleeping. Tower stopped when she moved into low breathing.

While she rested, Tower got on his personal computer. He softly tapped the keys and logged onto the website Shannon used. There were three new messages. Still, no messages from Shannon. On the computer, the short lines of communication all talked about finding 7Jud. Tower thought and could not figure out the identification of 7Jud. He scrolled through the messages and did not find that name anywhere. He now wondered if that was the hitman or maybe Shannon had changed up her name.

"Find anything?" Mason was awake.

"No. Just checking. There's nothing here." He closed up the laptop. "I know what she's doing?"

Mason was sitting up. She raked her fingers across her eyes and started to reach for an imaginary glass. "Normally, I'd be downing my vodka." She got up, went to the bathroom, and returned with a glass of water. "This water stuff doesn't have much punch."

"Better than vodka," Tower said.

"Yeah, but it won't take you anywhere." She drank half the glass and stared at Tower on the computer. "Shannon?"

Tower nodded.

Kinnie Mason let her mind wander. She wondered if she could keep the monster from the door. The pill monster. The pills were her friends. They did all the work. Once down, she could drift. Her body would be in a comfort zone of exhilaration and ecstasy. Mason closed her eyes and remembered the high. Creativity and free will evaporated in the process. She was willing to forgo the passion side of her, all for the demon pill monster. Yet, could she keep him out of her life? Sometimes, she could feel the monster close to her, just outside the door. Just leave. Get back in the grasp of the monster's hands, feel your inner being go soft. Let the monster do the heavy lifting. Kinnie Mason opened her eyes, staring at the hotel door.

"Stay away monster," she whispered.

"Say what?" Tower was deep in thought.

Mason said, "She's trying to draw all the attention to herself. And if Shannon stays on the run with this guy, he won't come after you."

"That's a dangerous game."

Mason punched the pillow. "Hope you don't mind, but I'm gonna try and get more sleep."

35

Routines. Max Kornread adopted them. He followed them. His life now, well into his seventies, was a morning to bed world of routines. His breakfast, late lunch, and light dinner were as regular for him as the daily rising sea tides.

Kornread listened and heard no sounds emanating from the house. He was way off his routines. The bindings on his legs were biting into his skin. Four times during the night, he moved around as best he could since his legs were numb from a lack of blood flow. His breathing was off with the gag still firmly lodged in his mouth.

Hands tied, feet bound, not able to speak, couldn't move much. Kornread knew the only thing left he had free was his mind. Free to think about his sons, and the what-he-should-have-dones. His thoughts flooded with the many chances he had to say he loved them and kept quiet. The chances missed to insist on a hug or make them stay just a bit longer for one last conversation. He should have done all of that. Now, he was too late and caught up with the reservations of did he do enough for them when he had the time. When he was free.

He looked across the room and the three bottles of blood pressure medicine on the table. Pots and Pans. When his wife was alive, that was the term he used to describe the pounding in his head when he missed taking the medicine. Kornread was now a full day without the routine of taking his blood pressure pills. The pounding in his head had started hours before. Without the pills, the headaches would start off light, then progress to full-scale earthquakes in his brain. Pots and pans. The sound of kitchen utensils clamoring together. The ramrod pounding made the task of thinking almost impossible.

The knife.

The blade was six feet from him, at times bending the filtered sunlight, sending sparkles of reflection against the wall. As promised, the Figure moved the blade closer to him. Kornread heard a noise sounding like someone leaving the house. Maybe he was gone. If he could just wriggle closer to the knife and turn himself around, maybe he could grab the knife somehow and start cutting. The hog-tie binding was loose enough, Kornread thought, to do the task. He considered one main obstacle. Where was the attacker? He had an increased heart rate. An hour earlier, he was given one escorted trip to the bathroom and perhaps his last one. Efforts to get his medicine were met with laughter. He had to work this out on his own.

Kornread jerked his legs forward with enough force to actually move his body in a direction toward the knife. The rope-tie gave him the ability to draw his legs back, then forward in a sling-shot fashion to propel himself across the carpet, a few inches with each try. Slow, yet the process worked. Kornread realized doing this made a lot of noise. He had waited perhaps hours before making the first attempt. He was now three feet from the edge of the blade. Two more feet and he would turn his body around and reach for the handle.

The phone rang.

Kornread stopped. If the Figure was in the house, the noise would draw him in. As best he could figure, this was the tenth phone call he had missed. He always answered when his sons called.

Always.

It was routine.

Yet, Kornread was not in a routine world. He was close enough to turn his body and get close. He had to stop. The cymbals clashing in his head, the over-the-top heart beat, and the struggle wore him out. He felt himself choking on his own salvia. The breathing just through his nose was causing a burning sensation. He was tired. Kornread allowed himself a rest. Get reorganized. For the first time since he lived in the place, he smelled the carpet fibers.

The knife was just a foot away.

Kornread's first try to turn himself did not work. The second and third tries were like the first. He got nowhere and he was exhausted. Another few seconds of rest. His eye sockets were hot pools of heat from the high blood pressure. On the fourth try, he moved closer.

"Ah, you almost made it." The voice came from above him.

Kornread relaxed his muscles. He waited for his captor to move into view.

"Are you looking for this?" The Figure placed the knife just inches from his face. "Since you want this so badly, I think it's time you get a taste of the blade."

Kornread thought about his sons. He let his mind drift off into thoughts of raising them, caring for them and the many fights he had to break up. Then, he felt his body tense up, as if that would protect him for what was to come next. A final show of resistance. He hissed at himself for leaving the back screen door open. Kornread closed his eyes and shut himself off from the world.

36

The burn.

That's how Tower described it to himself. A burn. He looked down at Kinnie Mason, her dark locks splayed against the pillow. The burn was his weakness for an aggressive woman.

Weak.

The ring, the vows, they should all be pillars against the wiles of a strong woman with a drive to step on a marriage and get to a man, no matter the strength of the bond between husband and wife. Tower had let himself slip one time. Just once. Weak. He reasoned he gave in to the burn. The feeling of letting the onrush of a woman bent on getting to him no matter what Shannon said or did. He almost lost Shannon. Kinnie Mason could run at him, naked as an opened flower and Tower would brush her aside.

He was adamant. Or would he turn weak.

In the weeks and months after Shannon found out about the affair, she locked the door and Tower slept in his office. He got a rare break many cheaters don't get; Shannon let him back into her arms. Another chance. Another slim opening to show her she made the right decision. Tower was confident he kicked Burn in the ass. He fought off the advances of Kinnie Mason and concentrated on Shannon, now missing and very much in peril.

Kinnie Mason kicked at her covers. She started punching the air, like she was fighting an imaginary foe. The kicks became stronger. The sheets were kicked to the floor. Tower moved to her side. Mason started yelling in her sleep. "Help him! Help him!"

She almost hit Tower with a swinging right hand. He grabbed up the left coming at him and pulled Mason into a tight hold. He had no other choice than to just hug her until she could wake up. "Kinnie! Wake up. Kinnie!"

She opened her eyes. Wild and scared soon became calm as Mason took in the room around her and Tower holding her tight. He started to let go. As he moved away from her, Mason pulled him back toward her, down into her waiting lips. Tower pushed his arms up and outward until he broke up her grip on him. He stood up and took three steps back.

"I need you," she said.

"You have me. Just, not that way."

"I need more. I always have. I just can't get a little bit. I have to have more and more until I'm over the edge and down the side of the mountain."

Tower said, "I'm with you. I'm here to protect you and make sure you don't mess up your rehab. But, I love Shannon."

"I can't sleep for days, and when I finally do, I have a nightmare." Mason slid her legs over the side of the bed until her toes dug into the beige carpet. "I keep seeing Barry killed. And I am standing by and doing nothing. I yell, I scream, but I keep seeing his face. It's like he's calling out to me to do something and I just stand there like a dumbass."

"You would have been killed."

"And then I saw that clerk killed."

Tower put the sheets back on the bed. "You did what you could. You contacted the police."

Mason wiped down her face with her hands. "I could have done something. Anything. Thrown something at him. Look for a knife. Instead, I just watched Barry die and I ran."

"The man was armed. He's a profession hit-man. You had no advantage. None. You did the best thing. You got out of there and saved your life."

"Some life. You know what I was really looking forward to?" She licked her dry lips. "I was finally going to inject myself. Yep. The needle. Why wait for the pills to act? Just mainline the shit."

"But you didn't. You're recovering."

Her eyes widened. "I had it all lined up. Five crushed pills, prep them up and into the needle. Instant mindfuck."

"The only thing messed up would be you."

"Imagine. That was my goal in life. Injecting my pills." She got up and headed for the bathroom. "I need a shower."

"No problem. You want me to go outside?"

She pointed to him. "You stay right there. With that guy out there, I don't want you more than ten feet from me." She walked into the bathroom, carrying a fresh set of clothes picked out at a strip mall four blocks up. Kinnie would have picked up more outfits, yet stopped short after two teens thought they recognized the singer. She paid and left.

While the shower was running, Mason poked her head back into the room. "You find Shannon. And that's an order. Or the next time, I won't let you go."

"I will."

Tower picked up the phone and dialed Mark David. "We have to talk."

37

A converted garage seemed perfect for a police station. The place had all the equipment to work on cars and there was plenty of room for six offices added on along the side of the building. Tower scanned the place and decided to wait outside. The building was close to the marina.

"The city is letting us use some of their space." Mark David walked out of the single glass door, covered from top to bottom in near-black window tint. "We're visitors here, but they're being gracious."

Tower said, "You know I'm not just going to go away. I think Shannon is near here and I'm staying."

"I understand." Mark David looked over Tower's shoulder. Kinnie Mason was staring down into a ditch, filled with bottom water. A fish kissed the surface, chasing a floating bug. "I would probably do the same thing."

"What do you have?"

Mark David's face distorted into a grimace. "You know I can't tell you anything."

Tower cut him off. "We're talking about my wife."

David's voice had an edge. "We're talking about six murder cases."

"What about the living?" Tower felt himself digging his shoes into the sand-filled dirt. He shook off his building anger and tried to concentrate on all the facts. "What about the court cases? Anyone squeezing the convicts to get some names? We still don't know much about the gunman."

Mark David took a police officer's quick glance of the block, before answering. "Takes time. As far as convicts, two died in prison, a third has a bad heart and can't leave his cell." David's face was busy with recollection. "Two others get no mail and no visitors. And five others in gen-pop."

"Anyone about to get out?"

"Not yet. They're going over everything to see if a message got to someone to do the contracts on these victims."

Tower didn't ask any questions about the computer found in the marina since he got to the website himself. The bond between them grew out of hundreds of arrests, investigations built on a hunch, and the double-up program. Double-up meant two officers would walk the streets of Stilton Bay. Community policing. Tower and David got to know the people of a certain area. They also got to know each other. All that ended when Tower's name came up in an investigation about missing money from the evidence room. The case was still open and the money was never recovered.

Tower asked, "How is the store clerk who saw him?"

"She didn't see much. He had on a hat, sunglasses and his face was covered in sunblock. And, his back was turned to her. That's why she just remembered the star on his wrist."

"So, she can't check mugshots?"

"Not really. But we put her away somewhere. Gave her a paid vacation. People who see this guy end up dead."

"Sorry to hear about your wife." Dustin stepped out of the building. Tower was surprised to hear Dustin sound concerned, rather than giving him grief.

"She's not dead." Tower's right fist curled into a fighting mallet, then eased up and took the olive leaf. "I mean thanks. I don't want to be in the way. I'm just a husband trying to get an update."

"I understand." Dustin stepped off, headed for an unmarked car. A few seconds later, the place emptied. The homicide team working the murder of the boater were all moving in the directions of their cars.

"What's going on?" Tower watched as David stepped back and away from him.

"We're not sure yet. We just got a call from a guy who can't reach his father. The man was supposed to be on a plane two days ago. No one has heard from him."

"And this might be related to the case?" Now Tower was moving to his own car.

David shouted. "We're just assisting since this isn't our city. This guy lives across the street from Shannon's rental. Where we just left."

38

Tower and Kinnie Mason leaned up against the car. A uniform was unrolling crime tape and spreading the plastic across the road, blocking any traffic. She squinted at the house, then used her right hand to block out the sun.

"Why the ambulance?" she said.

"Ma'am, it's not an ambulance." A firefighter walked by, and responded to her. "It's a fire rescue truck." The disdain on his face stayed with him as he approached the house.

Mason dropped her hand for a moment. "Normally, I'd be on my afternoon high. Pills for lunch, followed by a bottle of vodka." She now used both hands to mask the sun. "That's the way I reacted to anything. Just down the vodka, followed by the pills. Everything will be okay." Her words were dripping in sarcasm.

Tower watched the homicide team, Mark David, and Dustin, go in and out of the house. Another hour passed before David made a slow walk over to Tower.

"I can tell you this because we're going to pass this much on to the media." Mark David slowed his words as if formulating what he was about to say. "The guy's name is Max Kornread. Sixty-three. He's got stab wounds from his chest to his neck. Blood all over the place. A mess." David looked at the unfolding scene of police and detectives. "Something I won't be telling the press. The killer raked the carpet. There's a lot of blood but he wanted to make sure we did not get foot impressions in the carpet."

"Do we think it's our guy?"

"From this victim's front window, there is a direct view of Shannon's old house. A perfect place to wait and watch. We have no proof yet, but I'd say it's him."

"How did you get on to this victim?"

"His kids called and left like seventeen messages. When he didn't call back, they called us."

"Any sign of-?"

"Shannon? No. We think this guy was suited up. Crime techs have to check in, but we think this guy kept his fingerprints and contact evidence to himself."

"He has to be our guy," Tower said.

"Listen Frank, there was some talk about going public about Shannon. Full media blitz. I have my own ideas but I wanted to run it by you first."

"I'm not too keen on using the media right now."

"That's what I thought. Since she was once in witness protection, I didn't think you'd want to go public."

"Not yet."

David walked off toward the crime tape dipping in the breeze.

Tower took out his laptop and began hitting the keys hard.

Kinnie Mason stepped toward him. "Let me help."

Tower thought for a moment, then took his phone and handed it to her. "We know the victim's name and where he lives. Find out everything you can about him on social media. His accounts and check on the usual places on the Internet. Pull up his picture. Google his name. See what comes up."

Tower took out a pen and writing tablet from his glovebox. Mason was locked on her assignment.

While she Internet searched, Tower pulled up any possible arrest record for the victim. Nothing. Except for two speeding tickets, he was clean.

"I found his Facebook page." Mason shouted. "What are we looking for?"

"Anything that shows us any tie to Shannon. If she lived here for a time, maybe someone in this guy's family remembers. I just want an idea of what he looks like."

Tower searched for his homeownership records, and found he was a widower, father of two, a brother in the Northeast. He looked up and noticed a small crowd gathering near one of the police cars. Tower decided to push things.

"I'm a private investigator," he said to the woman. Tower reasoned, she was easily in her seventy's. Her all-white hair was pulled back into a tight bun. The sandals were covered in the same dirt mixture he found in the back yard. Her hands were covered with gardening gloves.

"What's going on?" She spoke to Tower. Her eyes were on the crime scene.

"Something happened here, but the police will have to fill you in. Do you remember a woman who lived here a few years ago? Her name was Rene Wilson, at the time."

"Yes. I think so. Her house has been empty since she left. But a lot of homes here are closed up in the summer time."

Tower posed another question. "Have you seen anyone go into this house?"

"That house? The one with all the police inside? No. I was just thinking about him."

"Him?"

"Yeah. Kornread. I knew him by his last name. Really nice man. I hope nothing happened to him."

"Again, did you see Wilson or Mr. Kornread in the last few days?"

"No."

Tower again turned his attention to the facts gathered on Kornread. In twenty minutes, Tower had pictures of him. He discovered the house was once for sale, and then taken off the market. The for-sale pictures showed the inside of the house and gave Tower a glimpse of what the detectives were seeing. Everything was on his laptop. He knew how much the home was worth, no liens on the place, and yearly property taxes.

"Thanks for your help." Tower thanked Mason.

Reps from the medical examiner were moving the body from the house.

Tower guessed there were more than sixty people lined up on the outer edge of the crime tape. The juxtaposition always threw him. The air smelled ocean-fresh, topped by a sprinkle of clouds and below, the vast Atlantic. Palm trees bent with the whim of the east to west breeze. One could sit and let the surroundings move mind and spirit to a certain calmness. A calm one might not find in the midst of a Midwest snow storm. Against that backdrop, Tower could not understand how a person would have the mindset to stab a victim multiple times, or use an ice pick to inflict a final act of marking a victim.

They brought out the body of Kornread. A surreal moment of people watching, standing in beach-gear and dark sunglasses. He studied the faces. For once, everything stopped. Police stood next to their cars. All conversation halted. There were only the sounds of birds chirping, unaware of the brutal circumstances.

Tower's gaze stopped on one person.

A woman.

He stared at the face. She was wearing a large hat. The sunglasses blocked her eyes and cheeks. Still, Tower was drawn to the face. Like a zombie, he took tiny steps forward, not really realizing he was stretching the limits of the yellow crime tape.

"Hey, can't go beyond that." The voice belonged to a young uni. He held up his hand to re-enforce his words.

Tower said, "There's someone on the other side of the crime scene that I have to reach. See! Right over there."

She was gone.

Tower searched for the woman in the big hat. Nothing could hide a face that familiar. He leaned into the yellow tape, pulling the plastic.

"Hey! I told you to get back."

Another officer, just a few feet away, probably heard the raised voices and stepped toward Tower. "Do what he says, mister."

Tower angled to look for the face. He searched to his left. She was directly across from him, but on the other side of the street. He moved to his left, scouring the front yards for any movement. He felt a hard press of fingers on his chest. "Sir, you're not listening to us. We're going to have to arrest you for disturbance."

Kinnie Mason was now pulling at Tower's shoulder, trying to move him back. A determined Tower, all of six-foot-three and two-hundred-ten pounds of mostly muscle, was not easy to move. He held his ground, plastic crime tape draped across his chest, with two uniformed police officers in his face. They were yelling. Tower kept looking. Where was she?

A slight movement two houses away. The back of her head, moving away. She was leaving. Tower looked around. If he retreated back and tried to maneuver through the back streets, he would lose her. The quickest way to her was directly ahead, through an active crime scene.

"Please, you have to let me get through!"

Tower stood, solid as granite. Kinnie Mason and two officers pressured, yet nothing moved him. A third officer was now approaching, his cuffs out and ready to be used.

A calm voice entered the picture. "I got this. Release him to me." Mark David got the officers to back up. Tower eased the tension in his body. He pointed to the other side of the scene.

"She was there," Tower yelled.

Mark David said, "We have to go around. I'll help you. Who was there?"

"We're wasting time. She's getting away." Tower's voice was beyond frustration.

"Who, Frank? Who is getting away?"

"Shannon."

39

Tower drove down the street and parked in back of the murder house. Kinnie Mason had the window down, staring into front yards. A police helicopter whirred overhead, a gift from the local homicide unit. They were using the copter for two reasons: look for Shannon and for any suspects in the stabbing.

Mark David drove his car down the parallel street. Dustin was also in his unmarked, crisscrossing back yards, public lots and small stores. They were tied to each other by cell phone. So far, Tower's phone remained quiet.

"I was on a helicopter once. Flew me in to an outdoor concert. 'Bout ninety-thousand people on blankets." Her eyes were straight up, looking into the Florida sun. "Are you sure about this? You say she was disguised?"

"Her hair was a different color, big sunglasses, hat, and wearing leggings and running shoes. But yes, I'd know her anywhere."

"And her car?"

"I'm not sure about that. Her own car was left at the house. Didn't touch it. She has to have new wheels. I'm guessing she tossed her cell phone. Unless she contacts me, I have no way of reaching her. Unless, she pops up on the website or sends me a text from another phone, or email."

Tower was scanning yards and houses with the eyes of a cop. The years of knowing how to look for burglars and thugs, were being used to find Shannon, like she was a street hood or hustler. He stopped at a gray-painted house with brown trim.

He sat in the car, staring at the home. Kinnie Mason was silent. Tower got out. "Get in the driver's seat. If something is not right, or if you see anything, take off. Is that clear?"

"Got it." Mason stepped out of the car.

Tower approached the house. A row of cherry hedge was a border between the homes. He stepped toward the back, keeping his eyes on the front door. No movement. He kept going. His slow pace brought him thousands of memories of searching back yards. He thought about a human hand he once found under a clothing basket. The find led to a body inside and eventually an arrest. Then, there was the kite found in the tree, with twenty bags of pure heroin found tied to the kite strings. Another arrest. And the Dodge that took up two parking spaces. The hood was still warm. Tower found the driver curled up in his own trunk, one of sixty cars in a theft ring tied to fourteen countries.

All of the searches came down to one thing; his gut feelings. He used his gut to determine what to do in each of those case. Now Tower's gut was telling him that the shadow that caught his attention was too heavy for Shannon. A homeowner? Maybe. Tower leaned against the stucco wall and listened. He heard the definite crack of a stick on the ground.

Tower pulled out his Glock from the holster in the back of his pants.

He knew he was on shaky ground. He was not a cop. No one told him to draw his weapon. He was not standing his ground. This was a shitstorm if things went sideways.

Tower gently looked around the corner of the house. Immediately, he heard footsteps running away from him. Tower gave chase. He jumped over two bicycles stacked against a fence. The movement was faint, yet he could hear hard running ahead of him. He put away his Glock and kept going. He jumped two fences, and realized he was almost back to the crime scene.

Tower stopped.

He listened again. No movement. Now he could hear the conversations of investigators just yards from him. The person he was chasing was gone. Tower made his way back. He again stopped. Tower looked and stared down the street.

His car was missing.

40

"Thanks for your laptop." Tower took the device from Mark David. "I've got GPS tracking on my car. I'll get the location in a minute."

"You think she's in trouble? We can get some units there in a hurry."

"Let me see." Tower took a moment to scan the screen. "It's not far from here. Just drop me off. I'll be okay." Tower handed the laptop back to David. "And no Shannon."

"Sorry." David tossed the laptop on the back seat. "We looked for a square mile. Didn't see anything."

"Thanks for checking."

Just before Tower got into the car. "I think there's something in that house."

Tower said, "Which one? Shannon's?"

"Yes. If our guy killed that homeowner, obviously, he was waiting for Shannon to show up. But he could have been waiting for a chance to break in."

Tower closed the door. "Did you get the search warrant?"

"Just now. Yesterday, they didn't want to give us a warrant. Said the possible connection to the murders was not strong enough. Today, after this murder, the judge changed his mind. We're in."

"You're in. I'm not."

"We have a team ready to go."

Tower said, "Will they let me in?"

"Not a chance."

"But it's my wife."

Mark David pleaded, "It's a murder investigation. They won't let you step one foot in there." David took a turn down the next block.

"I believe Shannon was headed to her old house, saw the commotion, and left." They were two blocks from the GPS location. "I just can't figure out why she won't contact me."

"Protecting you?"

"That's what everyone says. There's another reason. And I really believe something is in that house that Shannon wants."

Mark David stopped. Tower's car was a few yards away. Kinnie Mason was sitting on the hood.

"Thanks for the ride, Mark."

"No problem."

Tower got out of the car. Mason dropped her head as he approached. "I'm not worth a bowl of piss."

"The only thing I'm thinking is that you are safe."

"Yeah." She took a small piece of grass that was stuck on the hood and tossed it against the incoming wind. "You could be in trouble, maybe need help. And the only thing I can think about is stealing your car and scorin' some pills."

"But you didn't. You came back."

"It was my only thought." She slammed her hand on the car hood and walked a few yards toward the ocean. She took both hands, rubbed the small of her back and arched backward as if to push the remnants of withdrawal out of her body. The waves rolled up on the beach like liquid fingers massaging the sand. The sun was lower now, and shadows from a nearby sea grape tree left a dappled pattern across her face. "I was five minutes from a place. A place I know I could get some pills."

"Why did you stop?"

"I kept seeing the face of my manager. I see Barry's face and he's calling out to me to help him. Only I don't do anything." She got up and walked toward Tower until she was just inches from him. "I would be letting you down. Letting Shannon down. Everyone. It's time for that to stop."

"You keep saying that, but you keep stepping right up to the edge." Tower took the keys from her hand. "You know how many people overdosed last year?"

"I don't want to hear about it."

"More than car deaths." Tower walked to the driver's side of the car. "One more time and I'll be identifying your body in the morgue."

"Not me."

"There's a killer out there." Tower pointed to Kinnie. "And there's a killer right here with those pills. More stunts like that and you'll be next."

41

Tower positioned himself inside the restaurant so he could watch the doors and customers coming and going. Mason contemplated where to start on a chicken salad. A bowl of fruit was next to the salad plate.

Tower watched through the floor to ceiling glass windows, letting a fish sandwich lose heat.

Mason spoke up, in between munches. "I want my guitar." After swallowing, she continued. "Want to practice my song I wrote for Barry."

"No problem." Tower thought about her comment. "You want, I can get you to a stage. Private."

"Naw. I just want to practice in the room. I'm not ready for any kind of stage."

Tower watched as Mason ate with the passion of a hungry person, for the first time since he met her. He made sure she drank a lot of water, letting the body flush. She pushed the empty plate away and leaned back into the plastic cushioned seat. "This is the best I've felt in a long time. Now, when I wake up, I'm thinking about music instead of my next high."

"Hopefully, we can get you back into the studio."

She started humming the tune again, the one about Barry, then stopped. "You know, he once got me out of a bar at two in the morning. Took him a few hours to find me."

"He went searching for you?"

"Yep. Went bar to bar. Who knows where I would have ended that night." She looked out at the royal palm trees. Got me home. Put me to bed. I never even thanked him." Her fingers started to beat to a certain rhythm. "Could never get him on TV with me. He always refused to be photographed. Now, I understand why."

Tower tossed the food scraps and paper into the garbage and contemplated the next move. He thought about going to Shannon's previous home again and watch David conduct the search warrant. His cell phone rang. He did not recognize the number in caller ID.

"Talk," Tower said.

"Stop looking for me."

"Shannon?"

There was a sigh before she spoke. "Just stop."

"I have to see you. Tell me where I can meet you."

"Forget about me, Frank."

"Shannon, you know I can't do that. I'm never going to stop looking for you, so you might as well meet me and let's talk this out."

"Go back to Stilton Bay. Once you get there, I'll call you again."

Dial tone.

"Who was that?" Kinnie Mason brushed her hair away from her eyes.

Tower got up from the table. "We have to go."

42

"That was her, wasn't it?" Kinnie Mason sank into the contour of the car seat.

Tower said, "We're headed back. Then, we'll find out."

"What did she say?"

"To forget about her."

Mason smirked. "That's not gonna happen."

The car bolted down the road. Tower made the trip back to his front door in just under an hour. Before he parked, Tower circled the block a few times, searching.

"You looking for him?" Mason's eyes were clear. Her voice and mannerisms were normal. She appeared as clean as a first snowflake.

Convinced the house was okay, Tower parked and went inside. Kinnie Mason followed, just one step behind him. He went to the living room, yet he didn't know what to do next. She never gave any other instructions than go home.

Tower waited a few minutes. Then, he went to the bedroom. He looked inside her top drawer, pulled it out, tossed the clothes on the bed and looked underneath.

A cell phone was duct-taped to the bottom. Tower grabbed the phone. Exactly seven minutes later, the phone rang.

"I'm here."

"She's with you?"

"Yes."

"Okay. Drive to where we met. Took me awhile, but there is a car waiting for you. Make sure no one follows you. Write down this number. Mine won't show up in your ID."

Tower wrote down the number she gave him. "Shannon, is there anything in the other house?"

"They won't find anything there anymore."

"That means you moved it, whatever it is?" The questions spilled from Tower. "Will tell you more when I see you."

He heard loud breathing, like she was winded. When he did not hear a response, he kept going.

"Why didn't you tell me?"

There was a long pause. "Just trust me. I can explain more later, then you have to promise me."

Tower answered. "I can't promise."

"You have to promise to stop following after me."

"You're trying to protect me."

"Not just you."

"What?"

Shannon sounded tired. "Just meet me." She hung up.

"I know," Mason said. "We have to go."

Tower parked the car.

Mason said, "You met at the beach?"

"Yes. The wind blew her hat. I tracked it down." Tower was out of the car and looking for another car, the one Shannon left for him.

He checked a message, coming from a phone number he did not recognize. The text read:

GREEN CAR – KEYS ON TOP OF PASSENGER FRONT TIRE

Tower found the car. As instructed, he saw a green car. He waited several minutes before approaching, always looking for another person. The normal go-to-beach crowd filtered past them. He went up to the car and found the keys. Tower looked into the car. There were no papers, no more instructions. He walked away from the car, found a bench and waited.

Tower answered the phone before the second ring. "Now what?"

"Go into T-Town. There's a dilapidated building on Terser Avenue and Thirty-Seventh Street. Come there, knock once."

Tower put away the phone. Mason got into the passenger seat. He started the car and headed for T-Town.

"I remember this." Mason stayed low in the seat.

"Hope so. This is close to Jackie's rehab center. I heard you bought some pills while you were in rehab."

Mason let her head drop back onto the headrest. "That was a blur." She closed her eyes for a moment and turned to Tower. "Seems like a long time ago. That ain't me right now."

"You sure?"

The half-smile on Mason's face turned flat as an ocean horizon. She blinked her eyes a few times, then seemed to fixate on an imaginary spot somewhere just beyond the hood of the car.

Tower started, "If you're still blaming yourself, stop. The action taken against your manager would have happened if you were sober. It was out of your control."

The car turned on Tyler street. The Avenues were numbers. All the street names began with a T. As he moved deeper into T-Town, the buildings showed more ruin. Five decades of promises from the city remained unfulfilled.

A woman tried to angle her face so she caught the attention of Tower. A hooker. The woman broke off the eye connection as Tower got closer.

Mason laughed. "She probably thinks you're a cop."

Tower looked down the road. "Round here, they all do. Even though I've been off the force for years."

Tower passed Terser, and parked the car more than a block from the building. "We walk it from here."

Mason joined him. There were few cars on the road. They walked past a dry-cleaners and print shop. A small store was just ahead, full of small items and a section for eggs and milk. The door had a buzzer-button to let customers inside. Tower remembered the place from his patrol days, when armed robbers picked the spot four times as a hiding place in seven months.

Kinnie Mason inched closer to Tower, almost matching him step-for-step. Fourteen paces later, they reached the building. For Tower, this was another building for the city to tear down. On three occasions, he found teens splitting up the proceeds from stolen purses. Since then, the owners managed to board up the place sufficient to keep people out.

Tower went around to the side door. He knocked once.

"Okay." The voice coming from inside was hard to understand. Tower pulled his Glock and turned the knob. Inside, the building was a shell. Several walls were gone and metal studs and wires were visible, leaving the rooms with a skeleton look. The elevator was a long-ago memory. Ahead of them, Tower saw stairs leading to the second level.

"Shannon," he yelled.

No response.

They moved closer to the stairwell. As Tower moved, his shoes crunched on broken glass and pieces of wallboard. A few chairs were arranged in a semi-circle. The building had four floors. Tower had no idea where she might be.

When they reached the second floor, Mason started walked toward a window.

"Step back," Tower instructed. "Could be someone watching the place."

Mason moved toward the center of the floor. Tower looked for Shannon. A voice made him stop.

"Frank." Shannon's voice echoed across the near-empty floor.

"Shannon, are you okay?" Frank kept turning, hoping to get an exact location on where the voice was coming from.

"I'm okay. But Frank, you have to go."

"Shannon, where are you? Let me come to you."

"No."

The voice was firm and had a finality to it that made Tower put away his weapon. "Shannon, let me help you! Please, let's get together on this."

"Frank, just stay where you are. I'm okay and that's all you need to know."

"Just let me approach."

"Don't you think I want to be at home, watching TV all day? I miss it."

Tower started to take a step toward her, then changed his mind. "Why are you in hiding? Why can't I help you?"

The silence ripped through Tower. He moved in the direction of the voice.

"Frank, stop. I can hear you moving around. Stay where you are."

"Why?" There was no answer. Tower waited a full twenty seconds. He whispered to Mason. "The voice is coming from one floor up. You stay here."

"But she said not to move."

"Just stay here."

Tower moved as quietly as he could up the stairs. When he reached the third level, he saw a bed in the far corner. There was a battery-operated lamp and a chair.

"You're forcing me to leave here." Shannon's voice was no longer an echo.

"Where are you?"

"For the last time, stop following me."

"Just explain why?" He took a chance and stepped three paces in the direction of her voice. "Are you protecting me, Shannon?"

"That's part of the reason." There was sadness in her voice. "Where I go, death follows me."

"What do you mean?"

"My former neighbor was killed. I was trying to get back to the house. I saw you."

"Please, Shannon, let me help."

"No."

"Just give me a chance."

"Frank, I just wanted to hear your voice one more time. The man who is after me." She paused. "We all got caught into thinking he was one of us."

Tower said, "We can get him. Just work with me."

"It might be too late. Frank, this is all my fault."

"Why do you say that?"

"The deaths, they are all my fault. I can't trust anyone right now. Law enforcement. Others who left witness protection. I can't trust anyone."

"Why? What happened?"

"The information to track us down came from someone we trusted. And now, a killer is taking us one by one. There could be a leak inside our handlers."

"But you have no proof of that." Tower ignored an urge to run and grab her.

"Frank, you have to get away from me, until I sort this out."

"Shannon, was there something in the house. Something important"

"I already moved it."

"What was it?"

"Good-bye Frank. Too many people have been killed. Don't follow me, please. And do not contact the police. Just remember how much I loved to watch TV for hours. I will deal with this."

"Shannon! Shannon." Tower ran to where he thought she was located. He found two burner phones and a change of clothes left behind. The place had a back stairwell. Tower heard loud, hard steps, all going downward.

He ran.

While he ran, he kept yelling her name. She did not answer. Tower kept running until he was on the street. He ran a bit down the block.

Nothing.

He jogged back into the building, never stopping until he reached Kinnie Mason. She was staring at the rubble and stacks of crunched-up paper.

"You satisfied?" Mason said. "She's leaving you. Let her go."

43

Sam Dustin looked over the opened drawers and cabinets and let his shoulders sag in frustration. "There's nothing here." Mark David turned to him. "I just want to go over this place one more time."

Shannon's previous home was rearranged by crime techs. The search was going into the fourth hour. David looked out the opened front door. Across the street, the murder scene there was wrapping up. A red evidence seal covered the door jamb. A uniform was taking down the crime tape, then he would assume a spot in front of the house, making sure no one approached.

"Did you check the wall?" Dustin pointed to the wall behind a large chair. "Maybe she hid something in the wall?"

Mark David said, "We could get a pinhole camera in here and spot check a few places."

"Thanks." Dustin said. He asked David, "The other house offer anything?"

"No. No fibers, no blood so far, other than the victim. And no gun shots. He had no surveillance cameras. And the death was a stabbing with a knife, they're sure of it."

"Not an icepick?"

"No. Many stab wounds." Mark David stopped. He was absorbed in thought. "It could be that since the victim is not on the list, he was treated differently."

"I like your thinking." Dustin stared out at the back yard, then back at David. "You think Frank is holding back?"

"Could be. I mean, this is his wife that's missing. If it was your wife, wouldn't you keep some things to yourself."

"Maybe we should put a man on him. Follow."

"I thought about that. We don't have the overtime hours approved for that."

Mark David picked up a stack of magazines for the third time. "Something here is missing. Can't put my finger on it."

"We checked everything. Let's give it a rest." Dustin was walking to the front door. "You really think that was Shannon he saw?"

"Frank? Maybe. He believed it was her." He threw the magazines on the coffee table. "Okay, we're done."

44

Tower dropped off the car Shannon provided, parking in the same spot. He got into his own car and drove home. The entire time he kept rolling over in his mind everything Shannon told him in their brief conversation.

Tower walked into his home in Stilton Bay exhausted.

"You look like a zombie." Kinnie Mason dropped softly into the folds of the couch.

Tower whispered, "I need one hour of sleep."

"One? Honey, you need some hibernation time."

Tower leaned back in his chair, fighting the very sleep he desperately needed. "She said she moved it." He got up and walked around the family room. "What is the it she means? Think!"

He took out the laptop and logged into the message board site. Tower scrolled up and down the site, yet he was staring at the same old messages left on the board. The same messages he had discovered before. Still nothing new. "There's got to be something in here I'm missing."

Mason picked up the guitar resting next to the couch. She started strumming.

Tower rubbed his eyes.

"Sleep boogy-man gonna getcha, if you don't close your eyes for a bit." She was humming now.

"I have to keep going until I get a fix on what Shannon meant."

Kinnie started to sing. "I am sitting....sitting on the edge of your heart. Watching your love go by."

Tower again leaned back in his chair. The words were comforting, the soft guitar was soothing. He kept his eyes open. Then the blinking started. Each time he blinked, the edges around Mason's body softened, no longer in sharp focus.

She kept singing. "Wondering if you will ever come by. You are gone and now, my tears are falling up. Up. My tears are falling up to you."

For Tower, the windows were now fuzzy boxes, the melodic tones and velvet voice took him to a place of even-breathing. Her words were still coming at him.

"Grey clouds, standing brook, your voice is missing," she sang. "No way to slow down, a new time is coming. The journey is within me. Still, you are gone. And now, my tears are falling up. My tears are falling up to you."

The vision before Tower of Mason singing was now a wall of charcoal mist. He was no longer on a chair in his house. Tower was in the midst of a dream. He let the dream take him over.

A dragon with muscled and rigid plates along its side, thundered a growl, until it echoed far into the valley. The dragon's chest swelled and released a line of fire in the direction of a woman tied to a stump. She cried for help, pulling as hard as she could against the ropes strapped across her chest.

Her beauty was evident.

The dragon belched fire and landed another line of flames just yards from the screaming woman. A massive foot was raised and the dragon took a step toward her. The ground shook and the beast exhaled a wall of fire. A section of trees were reduced to burned out sticks. The dragon moved closer to her. She leaned back away from the monster to keep away from the heat. The dragon was close enough now, he could take her with a single blast of fire, or just snatch her with his teeth. The dragon turned and saw a man in full armor, shiny chest plate and a sword. The warrior felt his breast plates turning from warm to hot. Plants wilted and burned down to the ground. The man stood in front of the woman, blocking the dragon's path to the woman. He raised his sword and aimed the blade directly at the dragon's mouth. From behind them, the woman spoke. Soft at first, then he heard her.

"Help me, Frank."

Frank Tower woke up from his deep slumber. He looked around the room. "Kinnie."

He looked for her. She was not in the bathroom. Tower was the only one in the house. Her guitar was again resting against the couch. He looked out front. The street was clear. When he turned to the inside of the house, he saw the laptop was in a new position. He turned the thing on.

Tower read her words out loud. "I left a message for the Figure. I am going to him. Convince him to take me instead of Shannon. Please, do not follow me. I have to do this for my Barry and your Shannon. Let me do this." Tower moved to the front door.

His car was missing.

45

Frank Tower weighed his options. Panic was not on the list. He went back into the house and considered what to do next. He checked his laptop and checked the location of the car. Tower always kept a tracking device bolted to the chassis.

"Dammit." Tower let his fist come down on the table. The monitoring site showed his car was parked. In the same location where Shannon left a car for him. Tower reasoned Kinnie Mason switched cars and was now traveling in Shannon's gift-car. Tower had no way to track that car. Back to starting over.

For the next several minutes he went over every piece of evidence and everything said to him and weighed each item carefully. He again thought about the message from Kinnie. He clicked on the message board site and looked for any message from Kinnie. Nothing looked unusual.

Then he found something.

Kinnie left a message with her cell phone number. Tower pulled out his own cell phone and dialed.

"Hello." The voice on the other end was Mark David.

Tower said, "I need your help."

"Where are you?"

"At home."

Mark David's voice sounded anxious. "Mo is coming after you."

"Why?" Tower shouted into the phone.

"She thinks you're holding back, or rather obstructing."

"I'm looking for Shannon."

"She thinks you contacted her and now you're holding back, not telling us everything."

"You already know everything."

Mark David's voice took on a sharp edge. "Come in Frank. Talk it out with her. Answer her questions."

"Won't happen."

"What's up? Why did you call me?"

"Shannon is in trouble and now Kinnie Mason has disappeared."

"How did you lose her?"

"She took off while I was sleeping. But here's the thing. I need some help on your end. You have the ability to use all the surveillance cameras in the area. I am sure she got into a car at the park in T-Town. About an hour ago. You can track her."

"Okay. I can do that. What are you going to do?"

"I can't come in. I'm too close to something. They both need my help right now."

"I'll pass this on, but if she thinks you're hiding stuff."

Tower tried to remain calm. "I can't let Mo or anyone else stop me from helping Shannon."

"You spoke to her, didn't you?"

"I just need your help."

"What did Shannon say?"

Tower looked around the room. Shannon's words were burned into his memory. She said she had moved it. What was it? He had searched all the rooms, every hiding place he could at the house. He was convinced the it she talked about was in the house somewhere.

Something hit him hard. Shannon said she missed watching TV all day. Tower's thoughts focused on the comment. He looked again around the room. Watch TV all day. "She never watched TV. Hated the term binge-watching."

"Frank, what in the world are you talking about?"

"Mark, I'm just bouncing some thoughts off you. Okay, I spoke to her. Arrest me if you want. She spoke about something." Tower looked at the coffee table.

"Mark, I have to go."

Before Mark David had a chance to respond, Tower ended the conversation. All this time and the it was right in front of him. Shannon had given him a directive. A strong one. Her sarcastic remark about watching television was key. He looked in front of his television. Beside the remote control, there was something else.

A new remote. One he had never seen before. Tower cracked open the case. Inside, the guts had been removed.

Tower found a flash drive.

46

Tower fought off the urge to run out the door, without any direction and look for Shannon and Kinnie. He called the cell numbers he had for both of them, and got nothing.

He slapped a legal-sized yellow note pad on the table. Next, he inserted the flash drive. Within a few seconds, several folders popped up on his laptop screen. Three of the folders were named BEFORE. One was called NOW. Off to the far left, there was a file called PLAY FIRST.

Tower clicked on the file and discovered a piece of video. He hit play. The video was Shannon. He could not determine the background. The cell phone camera was tight on her face. He listened.

"Frank, I hope you find this. I am sorry for everything and for not telling you. This will be hard, but please do not open the files on this flash drive until I say so. Keep them secret for now. I just want you to hold on to this." Shannon paused, then continued. "Trust me Frank. I know that's hard because I didn't' tell you everything about me. But trust me now. Don't let anyone, and I mean anyone see this until I give you the clear. And that means you as well. Take care Frank. I love you."

The video ended.

Tower was a mass of divided emotions. His police background, his years of being a private detective, all told him to open every file and go through the contents. He wanted to know more about what Shannon was hiding.

A check of the time showed Kinnie had been gone more than thirty minutes. Tower felt the pressure to get out of the house and move in some direction, but where? Kinnie made it as easy as possible for the Figure to reach her, yet she would not pick up the phone when Tower called, unless Tower thought, she was in trouble.

Tower walked out the front door. First, he had to locate a car to drive. Then, move on a hunch, hopefully in the right direction. He was just about to pull out his cell phone and call someone, when Mark David pulled up in his unmarked.

"I caught you," he said.

"Good to see you." Tower approached him.

"Don't go anywhere," David said.

"I have to leave. And by leave, I mean right now."

Mark David got out of the car. Tower knew that body movement. The way an officer gets out a car with a target in mind. David never let his eyes roam away from Tower. He moved and stood in a way, as if to block Tower from walking down the sidewalk.

"What's this about?" Tower stopped all forward movement.

"It's not my doing, I just want you to understand that."

"Just spill, Mark."

"It's Mo. She's on her way here."

"Here?"

"She's coming to arrest you."

47

"It's this whole obstruction thing again?" Tower stacked his arms.

Mark David checked his watch. "Like I said, it's out of my hands. She thinks you're hiding a ton of stuff and unless you say the right things, she's taking you in."

Frank Tower had the ability to do a lot of things, yet since leaving the force, he had a hard time hiding what he felt inside. She was right.

David said, "You are keeping a lot to yourself. You can't be a one-man investigation."

"But it's my-"

"I know. It's your wife. And now, you've lost your client. It's getting away from you, Frank. Bring us into this. Tell us what you know. We can deal with this together."

"You mean, cut me out of this."

"She'll be here any minute."

"Then, you didn't see me." Tower started walking away.

"She's just going to come after you."

"Let her."

"Listen, Frank, we have six known murders. Maybe a seventh. Your help is critical, if you know something."

Tower tapped his front pocket where he kept the flash drive, as though it was burning hot. "I have nothing to share with you."

"Nothing?"

"I just want to get going. Can you give me a ride?"

Mark David looked around. "No car either?"

"Did you find out anything?"

"I did. I was hoping to convince you to go with me to the office, but I see that's going to be difficult."

"Mark, could there have been a leak? Someone to point out everyone who left witness protection?"

"That's out of my area. I have no idea right now."

Tower asked, "Can I see the files?"

"You know I can't do that."

"You have them on your laptop, right? Just let me take a quick look."

Mark David stood there, as if he was asked to give up his bank account information. "You sound like you're looking for something specific."

"I just want to take a look."

"You said leak. Is there something I should know about?"

"Mark, I'm just following a gut feeling."

"I could get suspended or worse, all based on your gut feeling?"

"Please, just let me see them."

"This gut feeling, where are you getting your information?"

"Just the files. Please."

Mark David pulled the laptop from his trunk. He cued up the files and handed the laptop over to Tower.

"What you are looking for?"

Tower read as fast as he could. He swiped from page to page. He never answered Mark David.

Tower handed the laptop back to him. "The first case, you discuss that at length with Mo and the others?"

"We did. It's part of the overall picture."

"Anything strike you as odd? Anything."

Mark David rubbed his chin. Tower reasoned he was trying to figure out what he could release.

Tower asked again. "That first victim."

"What about him?"

"That one stands out."

Mark David said, "His name was Evit. Evit Moark. Guy was the principal witness in a business kickback scheme. City contracts into the millions. Moark was all set to testify, but they all pled out. Six guilty. Moark was a victim of the Figure. Or at least we think so."

"What do you mean?"

"From the reports you just read, detectives went to his house. Blood everywhere."

"So, what's the problem?"

"We never found his body."

Tower stared at Mark. "I remember Crespo talking about that. So, how do you know he's dead?"

"We got photographs sent to us. Five to be exact. All pictures of his body. Two to the back of the head. Ice pick still in his head. We blew it up. A number one was on the handle."

"But no body?"

"Nope. We're still looking. But for now, Moark is listed as the first victim."

"And where did the pictures come from?"

"We don't know. They're still working on that. Frank, you've got to tell me why you're asking. Everything. Right now."

Tower stood, refusing to speak. Mark David kept silent. Two friends, former police partners, now both standing quiet as a park monument. A full thirty seconds went by. "I'm not giving in," Tower finally said. "Mo can do whatever she wants, I have to do something first."

"How much time do you need?"

"Twenty-four hours, that's it."

"And after the twenty-four?"

"I promise Mark, I'll spill. Tell you everything. I promise. Just give me that time."

"So, when you say everything, that means you know something right now?"

Again, Tower stood silent. Then, "Give me a ride."

Mark David gave him the look of a cop about to slap cuffs. "Where am I going?"

"Just drop me off near T-Town and I'll manage the rest." Tower got into the passenger seat before Mark had a chance to say no.

"What should I tell Mo?"

Tower snapped on the seat beat. "Tell her what you want. Look, what I've done so far, would you really arrest me?"

Mark David shook his head.

Tower pointed down the road. "Exactly. I'm looking after my wife and my client. So far as I know, that's not illegal."

Mark David started the car and pulled out into the street. "After the twenty-four, call me, no matter what. Is that a promise?"

"A promise. Now, get me to T-Town."

48

Shannon Tower flicked a mosquito away from her face and stared off in the direction of the camp. She picked a spot away from other campers. Stilton Bay Preserve was currently home to sixteen campers, all spread out near the Intracoastal Waterway, not more than a half-mile stroll from the ocean.

She was off the grid.

Shannon had no phone, no laptop, her tent was near the water and positioned herself to see who was coming and going. She had resisted dinner invitations from other campers and two flirtations from a passing park employee. She just wanted to be alone.

A walk into the deep shade of trees led to discoveries of raccoon tracks. The sun shone through the skin left behind by a water moccasin. Arrows of light pierced the trees and lit up the path for Shannon. The ground had a certain cushion, built up by decades of dead leaves and mud. All noise shut off as soon as she entered the realm of the tall trees. There was quiet, a stillness from the shoulders of the long branches. Shannon looked up and there was only the hint of the sun. She was wrapped in nature's blanket and she liked the calm.

There was peace here.

Her constant companions now were wild periwinkle, the sharp-bladed sawgrass and zebra-like Florida butterflies. She passed the shallow pond, home to a six-foot alligator and her smashed cell phone she tossed into the brackish water the day she arrived.

There were regrets. She had cut herself off from Frank. Twice a day, she fought off the urge to head out of the preserve and look for a phone to call him. Just not today. The walk in the woods was just the right thing. She found her new favorite spot. A tree stump made the perfect place to sit. Shannon sat and let Nature speak to her. The constant call from a baby bird filtered down through the branches above her. There was no wind, no rush of traffic noise, no din of restaurant clatter. Shannon took in a deep breath and wondered if she could stay there forever.

Still, she missed Frank.

Regret again washed over her. She could have told him. Just try and explain everything. Shannon shook her head in the shadow of a deep-rooted Banyan tree. She thought for a moment on what she would do for the rest of the day. There were boat rentals and one option remained strong. Shannon could move up along with the water line, exploring the protected mangroves. She would worry about dinner plans later. Shannon picked up a small rock and tossed it twenty yards from her.

Just as the rock landed, she thought she heard another sound. Shannon remained quiet.

Nothing.

She stood up and continued to listen. Then, a twig snapped. The silence was broken some twenty yards from her. Based on her knowledge and experience, the sound probably was not a Florida panther. If anything, the panther would move away from a human. A wild pig would make a ton of noise. She ruled out both. A full two minutes later, Shannon heard only the quiet of the reserve. She started to walk back to her camp. There was something behind her.

The soft crush of weight on the forest bottom. The feet of something or someone matching her own steps. There was a surge in her heartbeats. Shannon's breathing quickened. She picked up the pace. As she moved faster, so did the steps behind her. Now Shannon was in a full run. The opening out of the forest was still some thirty yards away. She could hear the heavy pick up and drop of feet behind her. She had to move faster.

The opening was just ten yards away. She forced herself to keep running. Her lungs were thick like they were stuffed with steel wool pads. Breathing was harder. She was tired. Shannon refused to stop. She kept running. When Shannon reached the opening, she stopped. Her body was on low-power. She needed rest. Shannon bent over and took in as much air as possible. She could not move until her lungs were satiated. Her legs were like sacks filled with sand.

She raised up out of the bent-over stance.

A hand wrapped around her neck and started pulling her back into the woods. Shannon tried but could not shout out to the camps. She had no air and they were too far away. She kicked away at something, anything, yet still missed. Shannon felt herself getting weaker. No longer able to kick back, she was again enveloped by the warmth and quiet of the deep woods. She saw a hand come up near her face. And in the hand, Shannon saw the sharp pointed end of an ice pick.

49

Frank Tower waited until David was out of sight, and then he walked two blocks until he reached his car. Kinnie Mason was kind enough to leave the keys in the ignition. He got behind the wheel and sat. Where was he going?

He was sitting in the parking lot staring at dead-ends. Shannon was not answering her phone and Tower wondered if the phone was still viable. Did she even have it anymore? And there was no way to reach Kinnie Mason.

His next move would have to be a good one. If he moved in the wrong direction, valuable time would be wasted. He weighed everything he knew, holding onto the knowledge if he moved too fast, he might step over a key clue.

Tower drove to the last place he had seen Shannon. He passed Terser and parked right in front of the building. He pushed open the door and listened. Hearing nothing, Tower walked up to the spot Shannon crafted a place to sleep. He searched for any sign that maybe she had returned.

He looked for new footprints or any food left behind. Tower kept a keen look for any movement. The place was quiet. The bed looked the same. Nothing new. He weighed his options. His only thought was how Kinnie Mason sent out a message on the Internet site in hopes of bringing the Figure to her. A simple plan, and also, very dangerous. Tower reasoned he could do the same thing, put out a message. He decided against that, since it might put Shannon in

danger. She warned him to stay away. How could he do that and leave her at the mercy of the Figure? He went to the window and looked out over Stilton Bay. Shannon was out there, somewhere.

His cell phone rang.

The number was not familiar. Tower answered. "Yes."

"I'll be quick. I have Shannon."

"I'll do whatever you want. Don't hurt her."

"She's not talking. At least not yet. She has something I'm looking for. Bring it, or..."

"Just tell me where to go."

50

Tower was directed to drive just outside the city limits of Stilton Bay, turn onto Bloom Terrace, the exit road out of town, then wait. He pounded the steering wheel. Evil thoughts poured through him, thinking about Shannon in the hands of a vile killer. Sometimes, not knowing was worse than seeing the truth.

The wait made Tower unreasonable. He got out of the car and looked for someone. Anyone. He thought he was being watched, then got back into his car and waited more. Tower logged onto the Internet site, but found nothing. There was no number to call back, as it came up NO CALLER ID on his phone. Even with a number, it could be spoofed, or made to look like someone else's number. Or the cell might be tossed.

Forty minutes passed, and Tower was a wreck. He tried to calm down. Getting all worked up helped the kidnapper. Tower rubbed his temples and let smooth easy breathing take over.

Three minutes later, his cell rang.

"You know the routine. If you called anyone, she's dead. If you have anyone and I mean anyone with you, I won't tell you where to find her."

"I haven't contacted anyone. I'm just here, waiting for your call. Where do you want me to go?"

"Go one mile down on Bloom. On the left, you will see a side road. The sign will say no way out. Follow it. When you get to the barn, park your car. No police and no weapons. Is that clear?"

"Is Shannon okay?"

"And toss your phone."

The conversation ended.

Tower held the phone in his hands, then tossed the cell into a grouping of wild periwinkle.

He drove off, his tires peeling in a cloud of sand and loose dirt. The speedometer topped ninety-five. He never checked his mirrors. Tower blew through four stop signs. His only thought was to get to Shannon. Now.

He slowed down, realizing he could drive past the barn and not see the sign.

Tower found the sign. A rust-worn square with four worn bullet holes made it hard to read, yet Tower could make out the words NO WAY OUT. He turned left. The barn was off in the distance. He looked for a house, but did not see one.

Before he got out of the car, he surveyed the entire place. There were no cars out front. Tower looked for anyone hiding in the scruff grass. Nothing. Anyone approaching was forced to park in a small lot, then walk a long winding path to the barn. A shooter could pick him off at will.

Tower put the Glock on the passenger seat. He rested his hand on the small caliber back-up pistol for a full twenty seconds, then decided to leave the gun in the car as well. He got out and stood by his car.

No movement toward him. He listened for any sounds coming out of the barn. The hulking structure of depressed wood was quiet. Two huge doors were closed. Tower started walking. The entire time, he kept his head moving from side-to-side, and back on the door. Still no movement.

One third of the way to the barn door, he looked behind him. His car looked like a lost soul on an island. There was no car traffic. No sounds of birds.

When he reached within fifteen yards of the door, he stopped. Tower looked for any sign of movement. Still quiet. He walked forward until he reached the barn doors.

Tower grabbed the latch and opened the door. He could see new interior walls were installed. Walls just ten feet away. The barriers meant he could not see all the way to the back. Instead, he had a view of twenty feet in front of him. From inside, the available light came from windows on the sides of the barn. There were also no fans and air within the place bordered on stifling.

"Shannon!" Tower called out. No one answered him.

Then, he heard movement. The sounds came from in the back of the barn, toward the right corner. He walked in that direction. Tower determined the place was a maze. The interior walls were all meant to block any direct movement to anywhere in the barn. Tower had to walk around in a certain pattern to get anywhere. And if not careful, he would get lost.

"Shannon, where are you?" Tower reasoned sound conquered maze walls.

The soft sounds he heard earlier were still coming from the same general area only louder. Tower heard a scuffling noise. He picked up his pace. Tower walked around a corner and found a dead-end. He backed up to his original spot and went in another direction. The sounds were getting louder. He started to run. Another dead-end. Tower retraced his steps and found a new path. The scuffling noises were now only twenty feet from him.

He finally reached the exact spot where he thought he heard the sounds. The room was a good thirty-by thirty. Tower was by himself. He turned in all directions looking for an attacker. He was alone. Tower's breathing was kicked up and his adrenaline was over the top. His fists were balled and he was ready to punch, kick, fight anyone within his sphere. Only, there was no one to attack.

The wall on Tower's left side crashed. As if released from its hinges, the wall tilted forward, then collapsed in front of him in a heap of dust.

Shannon was in front of him.

The fallen wall revealed another room, where Shannon was being kept. She was strapped to a chair and her mouth was gagged. Her eyes looked terrified and she was wriggling as best she could to escape her binds. An ice pick was angled three feet from her jaw. The pick was connected to a large metal spring with the spring tied to a braided wire. There was tension on the wire. Tower's gaze tracked the length of the wire. The cable was tied into a mechanism with a large clock. The clock was ticking. Tower took a step in her direction.

"You can stop right there." The voice came from somewhere behind Shannon.

Tower shouted, "I'm not going to leave her." Hearing no response Tower again took a step toward Shannon. The first bullet pinged off the ground near his feet. Tower stopped. A silencer. "C'mon out," Tower yelled. "Let's talk."

"Don't move, Mr. Tower."

"You talk, and I'll stop moving."

"Mr. Tower, I have the ability to bypass the clock and send that ice pick directly up into her head. Is that what you want?"

"I'm not moving. I'm here to listen."

"Good, Mr. Tower. She has something I want. And I'm very sure that item is now in your possession."

"What item is that?"

The second bullet hit just inches from Tower's left foot. Instinct made him jump back. He just heard a poof of the silencer before the round hit in front of him.

"We have no time for this. Give me the item now or she dies first, and then you, Mr. Tower."

"Show yourself. And we can talk."

Several seconds passed. Tower heard footsteps.

"You want to talk. We talk." The Figure was over six-feet tall. The silencer was in his right hand. He was wearing gloves. The Figure had cloth booties on his feet and the shirt was one-piece, long sleeved, with a zipper hidden behind a flap, neck to stomach. Tower imagined he was trying to minimize any physical contact and leave as little DNA as possible.

The Figure walked to Shannon, keeping the gun always pointed at Tower. When he reached her, he pulled the gag out of her mouth. "I'm not such a bad person. Go ahead, say hello."

"Frank, don't give it to him." Shannon's words were chopped, like she was out of breath.

"Ah, no words of love. I'm disappointed." The Figure held the gag back up to her mouth. "Tell him to give me the information or this gag goes back."

"Leave her alone." Tower was tempted to just rush him. By the time Tower reached him, Shannon would probably get the first bullet.

"Empty your pockets." When Tower did not move fast enough, the Figure pointed the gun again at him. "Move!"

Tower tossed his wallet and keys onto the ground, and tried to show his pockets were empty.

The figure reached behind the wall, produced a wooden chair and tossed it to Tower. "Now, put these on." The Figure tossed Tower a pair of metal handcuffs. "Handcuff yourself to the chair. I want to see it."

Tower did as he was told. He handcuffed his left hand to the chair.

"Sit."

When Tower sat down, he again took mental measurements of everything in front of him. As best he could figure, the Figure was fifty feet away. Beyond that, Shannon was another ten feet. The baseboard on two walls looked like they were on a roller, as if they could be moved in some way. The Figure also had an area out of sight where he might have things stashed away. A running attempt at the Figure would prove fruitless, unless Tower had a distraction. The clock mechanism was still running. Little time to waste. Above him, the roof was solid, however, there were plenty of windows on the upper levels. And Tower did not know if there was a rear door.

The Figure tapped a button. The clock stopped. "Mr. Tower, you have one minute to tell me where it is or I start the clock again. It's up to you."

"No, Frank!" Shannon wiggled in her bindings.

Tower kept the attention on him. "If you get what you want, you still kill us both."

"Maybe not."

"Let Shannon go and I'll give it to you."

"Frank please!" Shannon's eyes moved from Frank to the Figure.

"What does she have it on? Thumb drive?" The Figure lowered his gun.

"Maybe. And what makes you think I have it with me?"

"Mr. Tower, you were instructed to bring it. Not doing so will result in this clock moving and her death."

Tower stared at Shannon. He tried to read her eyes.

Shannon said, "Frank doesn't know what this is about. Let him go."

The Figure put his hand over the clock. "You have less than thirty seconds, Mr. Tower."

Thoughts and quick resolutions pulsed through Tower. The thumb drive was attached to the inside of his shirt. All he had to do is use his free hand and produce it, but then what?

"Nothing to say, Mr. Tower? Then I have no choice."

Tower said, "I know what you're looking for?"

"Really, Mr. Tower. And what is that?"

"You want to know all the information I have about Evit Moark."

The name made the Figure's face contort. "What do you know about it?"

"Stop, Frank." Shannon directed her words toward the Figure. "He doesn't know anything. He's just bluffing."

"Is that right? I want to know more."

Tower sat back in the chair. "Evit Moark. Shannon figured it all out. She said something on your little message board, didn't she?"

"Go on, Mr. Tower."

"For years Shannon has been collecting information. Not sure if she was correct, she kept it all to herself, putting everything down on a drive. But you also wanted more, isn't that right?"

The Figure moved his hand away from the clock. "And what would that be?"

Tower guessed, "You wanted to extend the list beyond the seven names, the seven kill contracts you had. You wanted the names of others Shannon knew about. Or else you were going to kill me. Isn't that right?"

"If you are bluffing, you're doing a good job. Yes, I wanted a new list. Those who left witness protection. I want all of them."

"And this Evit Moark, he's dead. I killed him." The Figure placed his hand over the clock. "You have sealed your future, Mr. Tower. A deadly future."

Tower waited until the Figure looked at Shannon. In that one second, he would move. The available second might be his only chance.

"I can change the angle of the ice pick. Rather than death for her, I can merely injure. I can let the machine keep hitting her again and again until she talks. I want to know everything. You're right. I want to start a new list."

The Figure moved toward Shannon. He kept the silencer pointed at Tower. "Don't move an inch!" Once he reached Shannon, he angled the ice pick in the mechanism so the tip would hit her chest. "There, now we can have some blood first." He walked back to the clock and was about to push the start of the clock.

"Stop!" The plea did not come from Tower or Shannon. There was a fourth voice in the space. A woman's voice.

The Figure turned his gun in the direction of the pathway. In walked Kinnie Mason.

"Don't kill her. Please! Let me take her place."

51

The Figure smiled. "Ah, we have a visitor. Please step forward. I was expecting you."

Kinnie Mason walked past Tower. Her eyes roamed over the handcuffs. She kept walking until she was just ten feet from the Figure.

"And why would you want to step in for Shannon?" A smile seared across the face of the Figure.

"I'm doing this for my Barry."

"Ah yes, Mr. Barry. Sorry to say but he is no longer with us."

"I saw you kill him!" Mason's words were filled with spit and emotion.

"Kinnie, where did you come from?" Tower tried to get her attention with the purpose of getting her to run.

She turned toward Tower. "I followed you. Stayed way back, but I followed you here."

The Figure's eyes moved from Tower to Mason. "And why would I honor your request?"

Mason's attention was again on the Figure. "Let her go. Put me in that." She pointed to the ice pick contraption.

Tower pleaded with her, "Mason, get away from here. Go! Now!"

"It's too late for that." The Figure waved his free hand. "Welcome. The door you entered is now locked. Believe me on that."

Mason moved toward Shannon. "Just get her out of that."

"Ah, Mason. I saw your post on the Net. I'm glad you're here." The Figure stepped away from the clock and hit a button on one of the walls. The wall rolled away. A mechanical sound filled the air of the barn. Once the wall was gone, there were now tables.

Tower saw what was on the three long-length tables and shouted to Mason. "Don't go near that."

The Figure spoke in almost a whisper. "There you go Kinnie. Everything you have ever wanted."

The tables were stacked with piles of pills.

Kinnie Mason's eyes lit up in a junkie's sheen.

"Go on, they are for you. In case you showed up, I wanted to make you welcome." On the tables, there were hundreds of opioid pills. They were stacked in small and large piles. Around the piles, Tower counted more than twenty bottles of vodka. Like a zombie, consumed with the passion to eat, Mason found herself walking toward the tables.

"Stop!" Tower stood up in the chair, still handcuffed. A bullet whizzed past his ear and left a small hole in the wall. "Stop moving, Mr. Tower. Let her hunt."

Mason kept walking toward the tables. She licked her bottom lip as if about to indulge in the world's greatest meal. She picked up the first bottle she could reach.

"Yes, Kinnie. It's all there for you. Just drink up. Take whatever pills you want. They are free, just for you." The Figure was smiling.

"I've never seen so many..." Kinnie Mason was overwhelmed by the amount of pills before her. She lifted one of the vodka bottles and placed the bottle against her forehead, feeling the coolness of the glass against her skin.

"Feels good, doesn't it?" The Figure was almost laughing. "I've got a proposition for you. It's very simple. You have a choice. You can change places with Shannon as you wish. Or you can have everything on these tables."

Mason put down the vodka and reached for the nearest pile of pills. She examined them, then picked up a few and rolled them around in her hand.

"Your old friends are back, Kinnie. Feast!"

"Kinnie, wake up." Tower was shouting from his position in the back of the room. "Wake up!"

The Figure could not keep his eyes off her. "I'll tell you what. Look what's under the cover."

On the table, next to the many pills was a simple kitchen plastic bowl. Kinnie Mason started to lift the bowl, then stopped.

"Go ahead. It's what you've probably dreamed about. Make the next big move. Do it, Kinnie!" The Figure bellowed.

She removed the top. And under the top was a syringe.

The Figure shouted, "Yes. It's all there. Everything you need to shoot it. Get the pill-thrill in one quick injection. It's all there, Kinnie. Forget about them. They don't know your wants and needs. Get it now."

Kinnie Mason picked up the syringe and grinned.

The Figure walked to the mechanism and again aimed the ice pick toward Shannon's head. "The snapping force will push this toward her with so much force, the pick will be driven up through her head." He turned to Mason. "You've made your choice." He pushed the button. "One minute and counting."

Kinnie Mason stared at the spectacle in front of her. She aimed the syringe at the Figure and threw it. "Fuck you!"

The Figure ducked away from the flying needle.

The movement took one second. Just one second. That's all the time Tower needed.

He stood up and rammed the chair against the wall, smashing the thing into pieces. Still cuffed to a small section of the chair, Tower rushed the Figure. He zig-zagged the distance between them and threw his body into the man. The Figure fired one round, hitting no one.

Kinnie Mason moved toward the clock.

Thirty-five seconds and counting.

Mason reached the counter and took a swing at the stop button, but missed.

Tower swung on the Figure, dislodging the gun. The weapon fell some ten feet from them. Now face-to-face, the Figure looked at the weapon for a millisecond, then concentrated on Tower. He kicked a bootie-wrapped foot toward Tower's face. Tower blocked the kick and swung again, just missing a jaw.

Twenty seconds and counting.

Kinnie Mason positioned herself directly over the stop button. The combination of the Figure and Tower bumped into her, causing her to fall. The weight of the two men prevented her from getting up. She tried angling her arm or hand to reach the button, but she could not.

Ten seconds.

The figure landed a gloved hand to Tower's stomach. Tower fell back, countered with a quick jab to the Figure's left cheek, then smashed a right hand into his face. The Figure dropped to the ground, off balance, then braced for a follow-up punch by Tower. Instead of landing another punch, Tower smacked the stop button on the clock.

The clock stopped.

Kinnie Mason ran to Shannon and started untying her. The Figure stood up and rammed his body into Tower, throwing both of them to the floor. The Figure got up first and got into position to stomp on Tower. Shannon had one hand free and worked to get her legs untied. Tower leg-whipped the Figure, sending him dropping to the ground. The Figure looked for his silencer. Before he got a chance to focus on the exact location of the weapon, Tower came down with two fists to the Figure's face and chest.

Shannon was now free.

The Figure tried to run. Shannon pushed him as he ran past, sending the Figure into the space once occupied by Shannon.

"No!" Tower shouted, and moved to stop Kinnie Mason. A wild expression moved into the Figure's face. He breathed heavy and seemed to ready himself for what was about to happen. Kinnie Mason thrust her body forward, slapping both hands forward, like a diver pushing off into the water, until she managed to hit the start button.

One second.

The full snap of the cocked arm was heard throughout the barn as the ice pick cut through the air and did not stop until the tip rammed into the slacked jaw of the Figure.

52

The jaw of the Figure was slammed shut by the ice pick. He opened his eyes as if in shock and tried to form a word. He began to moan, loud at first, and then quieted down. Then he went limp and stopped moving. Tower checked his pulse. Nothing.

"We have to contact the police." Tower moved away from the blood smeared device.

"I did it," Kinnie Mason was triumphant in her tone. "I didn't mean to, but I did it."

Shannon went to Tower. "I'm sorry. I tried to keep you out of this."

"You're my wife. I'm always going to be there."

"He promised he was going to kill you unless I met with him. I ran away from..." Shannon looked at the Figure. "Ran away from him as long as I could."

"The main thing is you're okay. But let me in on things. Even if you think there's danger there, tell me everything."

Kinnie Mason stared at the numerous piles of pills and the rows of vodka. "You don't know how much I want those pills right now."

Shannon put an arm around her. "But you didn't take any."

Tower checked around for a cell phone. He searched pockets for an identification of the Figure. Nothing. Tower looked behind the wall and discovered a large knife. "Glad he didn't have time to get this." Tower decided to leave the knife and let the area stay in good forensic condition for detectives. There was a line of blood on the blade. Tower thought about the homeowner's death.

He looked around. There was no phone.

Shannon rubbed her temples. "I just want a shower and get away from this place."

Tower reached her in a few steps and gave her a hug. "You have to promise me, if anything comes up, please include me."

"Okay, okay, I get it. I boxed you out. That was a mistake."

Kinnie Mason stared at them. "Finally. Together. What happens now?"

Tower said, "When the police get here, they will need statements from everyone. They will completely sweep this place with crime techs and take photographs. After a statement, they will most likely let us go."

"But I killed him." Mason stared at the body of the Figure.

"You fell on that button. Just tell them the truth." Tower was still trying to figure out how to call Mark David. They moved together and walked toward the way out.

"No one is going anywhere." The deep voice came from a man who had entered the space. He was holding the silencer. "I need the thumb drive and yes I know you must have it."

"Who are you?" Kinnie Mason moved behind Tower.

"I know who he is." Tower moved in front of Shannon and Kinnie. "This is Evit Moarker."

53

"You're supposed to be dead," Shannon had an edge of disgust in her voice. She broke from Tower's protection and stood out where Moark could see her.

Tower sized him up. Moark was not tall. There was a slight shake to his gun hand, telling Tower he was not comfortable with a weapon. His eyes darted back and forth, from the Figure's body to the trio. Tower did not know what was behind him. He only knew the path through the maze.

"Why didn't you do what he told you?" Moark took two steps toward them. "All you had to do is produce that list."

Shannon shouted to him. "And then what?"

Moark now pointed the gun at Shannon. "I have three buyers lined up ready to bid on that list. You know all the names. The list now, or I start with her first." Kinnie Mason looked unsure and squinted at the man in front of her. "Who are you?"

Tower said, "Let's end this. You haven't shot anyone. Just go."

"Not without the list." He kept the gun moving from Shannon to Tower.

Shannon pointed to the Figure. "The thumb drive is on his body."

"Go get it." Moark's voice was directed to no one in particular.

Tower moved back toward the Figure. "Let me get that for you." While

Tower moved in slow steps, Shannon kept up the conversation. "You were E.M. on the site. What happened? We thought you were killed."

"I was supposed to be the first victim. I convinced him to let me live, that we both could make money if we compiled a list of people who left witness protection."

"I trusted you." Shannon moved a bit toward Moark. Tower watched her. With any luck, she could block Tower for just a few moments.

"Trust will get you killed." Moark took a step to his left, giving him a clear view of Tower.

"We all trusted each other. That's why the site was set up. So, we would have a place to speak, freely. You destroyed that." Shannon again took another step.

Moark aimed the gun at her head. "If you move again, you'll get the first shot."

Tower pretended to reach inside the pocket of the Figure. When he came out with his right hand, he was holding the thumb-drive.

Moark smiled. "Good. Now, bring it here."

Tower walked in front of the snapping arm of the mechanism. When he reached the wall, he knew he had only one chance. Shannon took a step back, moving away from Moark.

The armed man walked two, three steps toward Tower. "Toss it to me."

Tower threw the thumb drive, making sure the small device landed well short of Moark. The shorter man bent down to pick up the drive.

In that instant, Tower went behind the wall, and produced the knife. When Moark looked up, the glint of the blade reflected in the sunlight coming through the window. Tower didn't know if he could pull it off.

One throw. The blade moved through the air without any sound.

Moark dropped the gun and pushed both hands toward the pain pulsating through his body. The knife protruded from his chest. Moark fell to the ground bleeding. Loud moans rolled up and through the barn. Tower ran to him and kicked the gun away.

Tower stood over Moark, then turned to Shannon. "Can you find a phone somewhere? Call Mark. We'll be okay."

54

"So, you helped run a web site for those who left witness protection?" Mark David sat next to Shannon Tower. She paused a moment. She cleared her throat. "I thought it would be a good way to reach out, not to talk about our cases or trials, but to just talk. Connect. We all went through similar things. At first, it helped. Then, the number jumped from just few to almost twenty-seven."

"When did Moark come into the picture?"

"He joined us a year ago. He didn't know everyone, just about ten. He must have used that information to form the hit-list for the Figure." Shannon smacked the chair. "I didn't know Barry Ruddup by name. He had a nickname for the website. We all did. But we were able to warn each other when the killings started. That's when I started looking for another place to live. To move away."

Tower said, "Sorry, I didn't catch on, but I didn't know."

She looked down at the ground, then back to Mark David. "I should have said something."

Mark David said, "It's not your fault. Evil feeds on good intentions." He smiled at Shannon. "And by running away?"

"I thought I could buy some time. Think of what to do. And the whole time, Frank was a target. I thought if they came after me, they would leave

Frank alone." She patted Mark David's hand. "I know now, that was a mistake. I should have called you."

Frank Tower joined them. "How is Moark?"

"He'll live." Mark David looked through his notes. "He'll be charged with conspiracy to commit murder. If we can prove he was at any of these murder scenes, he will be charged with felony-murder. He is starting to talk. Maybe, if we get lucky, he'll tell us who first hired this guy."

Tower stared at the barn, then turned to David. "Have you identified him?"

"Yes. The Figure, as we've been calling him, is Paul Deller. The star on his hand helped identify him. The star is black and might have been done in prison. We don't know yet. We traced him to some hits in Europe, but not in the states. Until now. He went underground for many years. And we still don't know who set up and paid for the first contract in this country."

Mark David looked like he was holding something back. "There is one other thing. Moark has the same prison star on his hand. He vows not to talk and it's still part of the investigation."

Shannon said to David, "Thanks. The reason I did not destroy the flash drive is because it could have the names of others involved. I'll leave that up to you."

The sound of Mark David's cell phone made him reach for his pocket. "Yeah," he answered.

David walked away from them and the longer he listened, the more serious the look on his face. He pounded the side of his leg and closed up the phone. His walk back to Tower, he kept his gaze at the ground.

"What's up?" Tower asked.

"Moark started to talk. He told our investigators he was part of a larger group. A group operating in and out of prisons. Says he bargained for his own life, then co-operated. Said he wasn't going to prison. When they asked him who was involved, that's when he attacked the two people in the hospital room. During the fight, something must have happened. Internal bleeding, I don't know. He dropped to the ground and they couldn't revive him."

"Is Shannon safe now?" Tower asked the question loud enough for her to hear.

Mark David paused before he spoke. "I think so. They know we're watching them. There will be a national jail search for the star tattoo. And plus, she's got you Frank."

Tower put his arm around Shannon. She smiled back. "I need a long shower."

"After we take some formal statements, you're both free to go. We already have a statement from Kinnie Mason." David started to walk off.

Tower said, "Good. We need some time together. And then, we're off to a concert."

Shannon pulled in close to Tower, "You're already used to the name Shannon. I don't want to go back to the other."

"Whatever you want."

Shannon looked up into Tower's face. "I saw you at that house. I came back to get a few things and saw all the police." She looked down at the ground. "I'm sorry about my neighbor. He was a good guy."

"Like Mark said, it's not your fault. This guy was coming after everyone."

Shannon stared at Tower. The remaining sparks of the low sun high-lighted her face. She twisted the curled end of her hair and for a moment, looked away from him, as if suddenly shy. When she looked up, her eyelids flashed him a few times.

"I'm sorry," she started. "We were supposed to be moving in a new direction of trust, after the..."

"After I messed up?" Tower finished her thought.

"Yes, after you, and that woman. It was me who made all sorts of demands on trust and then I didn't trust you with the secrets of my life."

"Operation Blue Dumpster."

For a moment, Shannon's looked surprised. She paused, and Tower detected the rush of thoughts now contorting her jaw.

Tower said, "Mo told me about it. Not a lot, but enough to know you saved a lot of people from losing everything."

Shannon smiled at him. "I did what I had to do. It was, be a part of it, or do something. I decided, I couldn't let people be ripped off. I contacted the authorities."

Tower leaned down and kissed her on the cheek. "So, do I call you Rene?"

"Rene is gone forever. I'm Shannon now."

"Okay, Shannon, it is." Shannon kissed him back. "I never should have kept the website from you. It's just I didn't share things, except on the site, I felt we all could share experiences going into hiding. I just didn't think someone would infiltrate the group like that."

"What about now? You said there are more names out there."

"There are, but I contacted all of them to go underground. The website is shut-down. Mark David and Mo know about them and I think they are safe. Just like when I first met you." Shannon grabbed Tower's hand and kissed his fingers. "You remember that day?"

"Of course, I do. The wind kept blowing your hat on the beach."

Shannon laughed. "I felt safe with you right from the start." She stared off at the collection of police cars moving out. "When we set up the website, it was just for us. A safe place. I should have known it wouldn't end up that way. And I should have told you everything from the day I met you."

Darkness swallowed the last few sun rays, leaving Stilton Bay in the gray grip of dusk. Tower had one last question for Shannon. "Do you still want to move away?"

The brilliance of her eyes bore through the deepening shadows. "I want to stay. We're in paradise, right?"

"That's what they keep telling me."

She leaned in and kissed Tower. "We have some catching up to do."

55

"I'm Kinnie Mason and I'm an addict." A smattering of "Hello, Kinnie," filled the room. Ten people were in a semi-circle, with Jackie at the top, leading the discussion.

Mason continued her stare around the group until she had looked all of them in the eye. "I know my mistakes. At least the one's I can remember before I blacked out. I know what I want to fight for, I know the talent I have and I don't want to waste it anymore."

There were nods of silent appreciation. The group was spilt, five each of men and women. Mason thought of one word when she first saw them all assembled. Tired. When you've been through a struggle, Mason reasoned, at war with yourself for your own body, the battles would wear down anyone. Once she announced her problem to the group, she felt stronger and a burden was removed. Every day since the incident in the barn, Mason reminded herself of staring down a pile of pills and walking away from them, leaving the vodka bottles unopened. She considered the moment just one victory in a line of temptations to come. This was the time to prepare for battle.

She started to sit down, then remained standing. "I have been on a terrible journey, with a chance to take the right path. I don't want to mess it up now. I need your help. I am committed to be here, learning everything I can to get better and to get healthy. And that starts in this room and in my heart."

She looked at Jackie. "I want to thank you for saving me from myself. I have a concert tonight, but I wanted to share my voice with all of you first, if that's okay."

Kinnie Mason started sing. "I am sitting. Sitting on the edge of your heart, watching your love go by, wondering if you will ever...You are gone, and now, my tears are falling up to you."

56

Frank Tower let Shannon move across the row first. They joined more than eighteen-thousand in a packed arena. The ushers made many of them leave their signs in the lobby. Some signs were short, WELCOME BACK KINNIE. Other signs had long messages written on them. During a lull, some in the group broke out, singing past hits from Kinnie. Outside, two TV stations were reporting on her return to the concert circuit.

A national TV network did a prep piece on Kinnie Mason, detailing what they found out about her days in hiding, rehab and the comeback. She was not part of the story. She made it clear to everyone that she wanted to make her first appearance anywhere, to be on stage.

The printed ticket did not mention a warm-up band. There would be no one to soft-sell her arrival. The electric buzz in the audience finally gave way to a synchronous clap. Thousands of hands kept an ever-steady beat. Four times a band member appeared ready to take the stage, only to disappear in the shadows. A lone microphone and stand stood in the middle of the stage. Every few moments, a person yelled, "We love you, Kinnie." The crowd responded with a burst of applause.

She paused behind the set and the curtains ready to reveal a giant photograph of Kinnie. She took in a nice breath, and let the moment stay with her. The pill demons were at bay and the world resembled a new array of colors, flowers took on their true meaning, all things positive were possible. The once cracked shell was put back together and the great sheen of clouded thoughts now showed clear. The crowd noise seeped into her adrenaline, and gave way to waves of confidence. She thought about the bird she saw outside Jackie's rehab center, flying with purpose and flawless direction. She was now flying in her own respect, on a new path.

There was no announcer booming her arrival to the crowd. Kinnie just walked out onto the stage. Her band stood and gave her an ovation. The packed concert hall also stood up and roared. She used both hands and gave a calm-down gesture. They cheered through the ovation, as if they had no intention of stopping. Kinnie kept waving hands for silence. When they were finally quiet, she spoke.

"Hi. Thank you for coming. As you read and heard, I've been through a lot. But I'm back now."

The crowd cheered again, and she again calmed them down with her hands. "I know I let you down. I let myself down, but that is over. I have too many people to thank for me being here. But I especially want to thank my counselor Jackie, and Frank Tower, who protected me." She paused. "I can stand here now and tell all of you, I am an addict and I am dealing with this every day."

There was no applause. The crowd stayed quiet, as though they were being let in on a secret coming from the heart. There was a long pause. She grabbed the microphone and held it close to her mouth.

"There is one person who is not here tonight. My manager. I think about him every day. Barry, no more standing on the balcony. I promise. I'm right here!" She paused again. There was quiet. Her eyes, once directed down toward the floor, were now staring off into the crowd.

"I'm going to start off with a ballad. Hope you don't mind. But, he was a special person. Barry, this is for you."

INVESTIGATION GREED
Frank Tower Mystery #3

They wanted to make some easy cash. Now they'll pay the ultimate price...

A vigilante serial killer carries out mass punishments in this pulse-pounding thriller about greed and revenge — the third book in the Frank Tower Mystery Series.

The instructions in the text message are simple: come to Stilton Bay Park, and you'll be rewarded with some easy cash. But when twenty randomly selected people arrive at the location, there's no money in sight—until they find a dead man, his clothes stuffed with thousands' worth of cash.

When they take the money, they have no idea they're playing right into the hands of a ruthless serial killer.

When the people who took the money start to get sick, they pay the ultimate price for their greed - with their lives.

It is clear that this "prankster" means business and It's up to Frank to track down the killer before they cause any more damage—but when another mass text is sent out, it's clear that they won't stop until they punish the entire city for their greed...

Get your copy today at
severnriverbooks.com/series/frank-tower-mystery-thrillers

AUTHOR'S NOTE

While my book is a work of fiction, there are thousands suffering from the grip of opioids. If you or someone you know is in freefall, please know there are many places where you can get help. The grip of the drug is both physical and mental, yet you can break free. Just take the first step, make the phone call or contact someone who can help.

ABOUT THE AUTHOR

For many years, Mel Taylor watched history unfold as he covered news stories in the streets of Miami and Fort Lauderdale. A graduate of Southern Illinois University, Mel writes the Frank Tower Private Investigator series. He lives in a community close to one of his favorite places – The Florida Everglades. South Florida is the backdrop for his series.

Sign up for Mel's reader list at
severnriverbooks.com/authors/mel-taylor